"Stephanie Berget has mastered the art of
writing engaging stories with oh-so-hot cowboy heroes. I've
been a fan of Stephanie's books since reading her first one,
Dancing Creek Ranch."
—*Sandra Owens, Author of the bestselling
K2 Special Services series.*

# GIMME SOME SUGAR

### SUGAR COATED COWBOYS-BOOK 1

## STEPHANIE BERGET

STEPHANIE
BERGET

*For my husband, my original cowboy hero.*

L osing her father when she was eleven was the first black pearl in a string of bad luck that had dogged Cary Crockett's life.

But that was about to change.

Cary fixated on slicing ice-cold butter into the flour mixture. Thinking about the past never got her anywhere. Her father was gone, and no matter how she rolled things over in her mind, she couldn't change the fact that she hadn't heard from her mother in ten years.

The day she'd graduated high school, Cary's mother had congratulated her on becoming an adult, handed her a graduation card containing one hundred and fifty dollars and informed Cary she was leaving. Poor children in some tiny, destitute country in eastern Africa apparently needed her more than Cary. "You're lucky you were born in the land of plenty, honey."

Cary knew her mother had never been very interested in day-to-day life with her daughter. Unlike her friend's mothers, most of who doted on their children, her mom was only focused on saving the unprotected and impoverished.

"Do you have to go now?" Cary's hands stretched out in a desperate attempt to change her mother's mind.

Her mother had tugged her hand free from Cary's grasp then gave her a hug and patted her cheek. A stricken Cary watched as the only person left in her immediate family took a couple of steps away before stopping to look over her shoulder. "Love you, baby girl."

Cary believed her mother loved her in her own self-centered way. But, such knowledge had done nothing to ease the worry of having only one hundred and fifty-seven dollars to her name, or the panic that had risen to the surface when she realized she'd have no place to call home in two weeks when the rent ran out.

She shook herself. Time to return to the present and the pastry she was preparing at Chez Romeo. Years of hard work and saving every extra penny had brought her so close to her dream she could reach out and taste the sweetness of becoming a pastry chef. From the first time she'd watched Ace of Cakes, she'd wanted to serve up luxurious desserts like Duff Goldman.

A frosting coated spatula zinged across the room, missing her head by a few inches. "Crockett, get your ass in gear." Across the counter loomed the angry face of the head baker, Moonpie-round and flushed red. She knew what was coming. One of these days, during a vocal attack on his employees, Larry, or Luigi as he insisted on being called, would fall down stone dead of a heart attack.

And she wouldn't be very sorry.

The man was insufferable, but in less than a year, she'd have saved enough to enroll in the Culinary Institute of America. Her dream was close to coming true. She'd already been researching apartments in Hyde Park, N.Y. She took a quick glance at her oversized watch. Fifteen minutes left in her shift.

Placing the mini blueberry Galette in the center of the stark white plate, she smiled at the sight of the perfect golden, flaky crust. After dusting confectioner's sugar over the fruit, she drizzled lemony whipped cream over the pastry. Several bits of lemon peel and two curls of dark chocolate on top finished the presentation.

At the sound of voices in the back room, she turned to see her best friend tying an apron over her clothes. She'd met Pansy Lark eight years ago at a local barbeque bake-off. The prize had been a one hundred-dollar bill, and that was money Cary couldn't pass up. It had been an effort in futility.

Pansy had won the grand prize, and Cary had come in last. Give that woman any kind of meat and she'd have you under her thumb, but she couldn't hold a candle to Cary's desserts.

Pansy's wig of choice today was a Marilyn Monroe duplicate. With her bright red lipstick and pouty lips, she was a passable double. Cary smiled. The eccentric woman had become the sister she'd never had, and the friend she'd always needed.

Cary dusted off her hands and pulled at the apron ties around her waist. Her eight-hour shift had crawled by with the speed of a crippled slug, but at last, it was time to go home.

"Thank god you're here. Maybe you'll make our prima donna happy," Cary said as she unbuttoned her chef's jacket and turned toward her friend.

Luigi beamed at the diminutive woman who'd just arrived. The maître de picked a new favorite each week, and everyone else received the insults he doled out like a retiree did candy at Halloween.

As Cary walked by Pansy, she touched her arm. "Be careful. He's been praising Benny all day."

Pansy gave her a weak smile. "I knew it was coming. Have a good evening."

Grabbing her sweater, Cary stepped into the alley behind the restaurant. An overflowing dumpster gave off the stench of rotting vegetables, but after enduring Larry's manic kitchen, the warm night air soothed her frayed nerves. Only a few more months of putting up with Luigi, and she'd have enough money to pursue her dream. She could do this.

She took a deep breath and set off the six blocks to her tiny apartment. The movement loosened her tight shoulders and relaxed her cramped legs. By the time she reached home, she felt better than she had in weeks. A sense of well-being settled like sunshine on her shoulders.

She counted each one of the thirteen steps up to her front stoop. Fishing her ring of keys from her bag, she reached for the doorknob. Her smile faded as she saw that the door was open a crack. She'd locked it when she'd left for work. Well, she was almost positive she'd locked it, but she'd been a little late and a lot frazzled.

Her nervous gaze swept to the apartment below hers. She could go to her landlord's and call the police.

*Don't be an idiot, Crockett. You forgot.* That was it. She'd forgotten and the neighbor kid had come in to look around —again.

As she stepped through the doorway, she reached for the light switch. A hand grabbed her by the back of the neck, and an arm wrapped around her waist. Smashed against a rock-hard chest, she struggled to breathe through her fear.

When she tried to scream, the hand left her neck and closed over her mouth.

Panic raced through her veins like a hurricane, blanking out her mind and weakening her muscles. She tried to pull air into her oxygen-starved lungs. When the grasping hands released her, her knees gave out. Blackness closed in on her as fear claimed her reflexes, and she dropped to the floor.

Curling into a fetal position would be the easiest thing to do, but she couldn't afford to pass out. As she scrambled to her knees, a light, bright and glaring, shone into her eyes. The blinding flash made it impossible to see who else was in the room.

"Hullo, Cary love." Although the pitch of the voice was high enough to be a woman's, Cary stiffened as she recognized the ominous tone. In her mind she could see the pale skin and sparse, yellow strands of hair, see his thin fingers and large rings. The hair on the back of her neck stood on end as it had when she'd met the man almost six months earlier.

Someone lifted her to her feet, keeping hold of her upper arm.

She pulled herself together and feigned a confidence she didn't come close to feeling. Jerking her arm loose, she raised her hand to try to shade her eyes. "This is pretty dramatic even for you, Mad Dog. You could have called." Despite her terror, she almost laughed when she called him Mad Dog.

One of her thrift store table lamps clicked on, and she saw the pale man nod to his accomplice. The brute moved away to lean against the door.

Cary crossed her living room and stood behind a straight-backed chair. The flimsy piece of furniture wouldn't be any protection if Mad Dog gave any signal for his hired hooligan to come after her, but it gave her a smidgen of confidence, and she needed all she could muster. She raised her chin and shifted her gaze back to the pint-sized thug.

"I didn't mean to scare you." Mad Dog took out a large white handkerchief and spread it on her sofa. He lowered himself onto the cloth, crossing one leg over the other knee. His smug smile sickened her. "Well, yes, I did."

She moved to the front of the chair and sat down. It wouldn't do for her to collapse in front of these men. "Did you want something in particular, or are you just having a few laughs at my expense?"

Mad Dog giggled then stopped to light a thin, brown cigarillo. He stared at the smoke as it curled toward the ceiling before turning his attention toward her, not saying a word. The silence scared her more than the big man's touch.

With the swiftness of an adder's strike, Mad Dog moved across the room and stood behind her chair. As she trembled, he ran his fingers through her white blonde strands. "Pretty."

It took everything she had to not jerk away. This man got a kick out of causing fear and any show of it encouraged him.

"Where is Ken?" His words held a conversational tone as he separated a lock of her hair and wound it around his fingers.

"I don't know." She couldn't contain the shudder that coursed through her body. She hadn't seen Ken since she'd chased him out of her apartment with a steak knife three months earlier. She'd thought she was rid of the bastard for good.

Mad Dog's fingers tangled in her hair, and he yanked her head back. As he held her in place, he blew a lungful of smoke at her face. "Do you want to think about your answer again?"

"Yes, I haven't. . . seen him. . . Haven't seen him for months." The smoke poured into her nose, and her lungs seized. Coughs wracked her body, but the sick bastard didn't let go of her hair.

As she watched, his face transformed from criminal to choirboy, but she knew better than to believe he was happy with her answer. He was a narcissistic psychopath, and he had her where no one would hear her if she screamed— when she screamed. "I want you to get a message to him."

"I can't. See, we broke up. I threw the jerk out." She babbled and couldn't make herself stop. "He stole my savings, and I threatened him with the loss of his—."

Mad Dog's face curved into the first real smile she'd ever seen from the man. "He stole from me, too."

She felt a tiny frisson of hope as she lifted her gaze to his. Maybe they could bond over their hatred of Ken.

His deadly expression froze her in place. "You tell him I want my stuff back." The ice blue color of his eyes matched the coldness of his heart.

When she tried to nod, he grabbed her chin and held her motionless, staring into her eyes as he spoke. "And just to make sure you know I'm serious—" Without looking away, he ground the glowing tip of the thin cigar into her upper arm and held it there as she struggled.

Her screams drowned out the rest of his words.

MICAH STOOD at the counter of the Five And Diner as aggravated as he'd ever been in a life filled with aggravation. He was offering Cal twice the money the man made here, and the cook wouldn't even consider his job offer.

Even after half a day of cooking over a grill, the cook's T-shirt was snowy white. The man was a magician, and Micah needed him. "It's only for a couple of weeks? I'm sure it won't take long to find a new cook."

Cal stared at Micah like he was an addle-brained calf. Without a word, he turned and filled Micah's oversized, insulated mug with steaming hot coffee.

Micah pulled out his wallet and held out all the cash he had with him. "There's a bonus up front."

"Keep your money. Them cowboys yell if everythin' ain't just so. I don't need that kind of aggravation." Cal turned his back and wandered into the kitchen, effectively ending the conversation. Before Micah could move, the cook stuck his head out the swinging door. "You better not let Lorna hear you tried to hire me away. She'll skin you for sure."

The rancher slapped his palms on the worn Formica. Years of scrubbing the countertops left little of the original color, maybe yellow. What the hell was he going to do now? The ranch hands would give him a couple of days to find a new camp cook, but they wouldn't tolerate sandwiches for long. They worked hard and deserved a good substantial meal.

Without ranch hands, he couldn't get the hay baled or tend to the cattle. Without hands, he'd lose the ranch. Born and raised on the Circle W, Micah intended to die there.

He wracked his brain. There had to be another person in East Hope, Oregon who could help him out, but who? A gentle hand touched his arm.

"Maybe I can help."

Snapping his head up, he whirled around, almost elbowing the woman standing behind him. Pulling in a deep, slow breath, partly to gather some semblance of calm and partly to adjust to the tingle where her hand met his arm, he took a step back before speaking.

"Help me with what?" Did he know her? He was sure he didn't, but man . . .

"I'm sorry. I didn't mean to eavesdrop, but I heard you say you're looking for a cook." Golden eyes the color of whiskey stared into his. "I cook."

He let his gaze wander over her, liking what he saw. She wasn't a local. Her white blonde hair was as short as a man's on the sides and curled longer on the top and back. He hadn't seen any woman, or anyone at all who wore their hair like this. Of course, tastes of the people of East Hope ran to the conservative.

Despite the severe hairstyle, she was pretty. Beyond pretty. Leather pants showed off her soft curves, miniature combat boots encased her small feet and a tight tank top enhanced her breasts.

When she cleared her throat, he jerked his eyes up to her face. "It won't do you any good to talk to my boobs. Like most women, it's my brain that answers questions."

A smart ass and she'd caught him red-handed. His cheeks warmed. Damn it, he was blushing. This woman was not at all what he needed. Time to end this. "I have a ranch, the Circle W. We need a camp cook. A man."

Her eyes narrowed, and her body tensed. "It looks like you need any kind of cook you can get." She held her hand out, indicating the empty café. "Not a lot of takers."

She had him there. His gut told him he would regret this, but she was right. He had no choice. "I'll hire you week to week." When she nodded, he continued. "I've got seven ranch hands. You'll cook breakfast and dinner and pack lunches Monday through Friday and serve Sunday dinner to the hands by six o'clock."

She bounced on the toes of her feet until she noticed him watching her then she pulled on a cloak of calm indifference. "You won't regret this."

He felt a smile touch the corners of his mouth as his gut twisted. "I already do."

She held out her hand. "I'm Cary Crockett." Her nails were short and sparkly pink, and she had a huge letterman's ring on the first finger of her right hand.

It took him a minute to realize he hadn't answered her. "Micah West."

His hand dwarfed hers when they shook, her skin warm and soft. For a moment, he tightened his grip to keep her from pulling away then he caught himself. No matter how charming a picture she made, he didn't want or need a woman. He cleared his throat then turned to the man who'd entered the cafe. "This is Clinton Barnes."

The normally reserved Barnsey chatted with Cary like he'd known her for a decade.

They'd be here all day if he didn't do something. "We've got groceries to buy," he said, his voice gruff. Turning, he strode across the street to the East Hope Foodtown.

Millie Hanson had owned the grocery for twenty-two years, the first twelve with her husband. After Mike died of a heart attack, she'd kept on alone. Micah had made it a practice to buy from her whenever he could. Because Foodtown was the only place to buy food and staples for forty miles, it was expensive, but friends helped friends.

He waited in front of the meat counter until the owner strode out of the storeroom. "Need to pick up the supplies I ordered last week." He glanced at the new cook. "And order some other things."

"Micah!" Millie walked right up to him, wrapped her arms around his waist and gave him a hug. For a woman on the far side of forty, she was something. Millie had more than a passing resemblance to Katey Sagal, and a body a much younger woman would envy. Her deep, dark red hair was striking with her pale skin.

"It's been too long since you came to see me. I've missed our lunches." She handed him a small brown paper bag.

Micah looked inside to find at least a pound of chocolate-covered raisins. "You keep spoiling me with my favorite candy, and I'm going to have to marry you."

Millie rose to her tiptoes and gave him a kiss on his cheek.

"Not if I get to her first." Clinton Barnes moved forward and threw his arm over Millie's shoulder.

Millie's wide smile faded as she caught sight of Cary. "Who's this?" Her expression told Micah she'd noticed the strange appearance of the woman and didn't like her a bit. "New girlfriend?"

God, no! All he needed was a rumor to spread through town about his moving a woman onto the ranch. "No, she's my new temporary cook, Cary Crockett. Cary, this is East Hope's number one citizen, Millie McFarland."

The look Cary gave Millie said she didn't care if the woman liked her looks or not. With a short nod, the younger woman acknowledged the introduction.

"Must be from San-fran-cisco, from the looks of you. City girl!" Millie almost spat the last two words as she made her way from beneath Clinton's arm. She took Micah's hand. "Come on back here. I've got your stuff all ready."

A slight blush raced across Cary's cheeks, but her expression didn't change. Before Millie could lead Micah away, Cary said, "I'm from back east." She turned to Micah. "Do your ranch hands like dessert?"

"They'll eat just about anything that isn't still alive." Micah watched as she drew in a short breath then breathed out slowly.

"Okay then." She bit her lower lip. He thought she would say more, but she remained silent.

"The boxes are in the back room. Help me, Micah?" Without another word, Millie was out the back door.

"I'll help her," Clinton Barnes said and disappeared after Millie.

Micah turned to Cary. "Look through the boxes and get whatever else you need. Charge it to the Circle W."

He turned and walked to the front of the store, his mood darkening. Throwing this pretty young thing in with the ranch hands was a recipe for disaster. That was a deep-fried fact. She couldn't even stand up to Millie. But maybe she would buy him enough time to find someone else. He crossed the street, heading toward the bank, his thoughts returning to the problem at hand.

He'd known he shouldn't have loaned Cookey two hundred dollars when he'd asked, but the man had been a good employee for over three years. It just hadn't occurred to Micah that Cookey would run off with the mayor's daughter. Hadn't occurred to the mayor either.

If the elopement hadn't cost him his camp cook, Micah would have been relieved. Mayor Juggs and Julie had been plotting to get Micah to marry her since she'd turned seventeen.

Micah sighed. Even if he wanted to, Cookey couldn't come back now. Mayor Juggs would tan his hide and nail it to the front of the town hall. A ranch cook was twelve stories below the husband Mayor Juggs wanted for Julie.

Unease swept through Micah's veins like a janitor on meth. He figured he'd made a mistake hiring a complete stranger, and a woman at that, but for the life of him, he didn't see an alternative. For the twenty thousandth time, he wished Marlene had wanted to be a ranch wife. His ex-wife had been gone for three years, only showing up a few times to visit with their daughter.

He cleared his throat and shrugged his shoulders. No use crying over spilt milk as his grandmother used to say. A short visit with the banker, and he'd be ready to head back out to the Circle W.

"Micah, how are things going?" Hank Loveland stood and moved from behind his desk. One Loveland or another had run the East Hope Bank since 1952. Hank had returned from Seattle ten years ago to take over the business.

"Good, I'm good. You said the operating loan papers would be ready to sign today." He reached out and shook Hank's hand.

"Have a seat." Hank rummaged through the papers scattered on his desktop and picked one up. "They aren't quite ready."

Micah's heartbeat hit double time. He didn't need more problems today. He pasted a smile on his face and waited as Hank looked over the sheet. "What's wrong?"

"I'd like to run your application by the bank's board of directors." Hank lowered himself into his oak chair, placed the papers on the desk in front of him, and leaned back. With the movement, a loud squeal filled the room. "A minor detail."

*Here we go again.* Everyone still thought of him as Big Jim West's little grandson even though the old man passed away almost a year ago. Micah stood and stuffed his hands in his pockets. "You never ran anything by the board when Pops was alive. Why now?"

"It's not that I don't trust you." Hank wiggled his manicured fingers and waited for a response.

Micah glared at the banker before turning on his heel and walking to the door. He stopped with his hand on the knob and looked over his shoulder. "You either give me the loan or I'll go to another bank."

"Now, now. Don't get mad. I'll—"

Micah shut the door on Hank Loveland's words with a soft click. He wanted to slam it, but that kind of behavior wasn't in his character. Walking out on the blustering man brightened his day.

He felt marginally better until he noticed the woman leaning into the bed of his pickup, settling grocery boxes into the back. Her bright white hair gleamed in the sunshine. The sight of her leather wrapped legs and ass, holy shit! He was enjoying the view when reality slapped him upside the head.

What was he doing hiring her? He knew it was a bad move, but desperation made a man do strange things. There was nothing he could do about it now. He'd keep looking and as soon as he found a suitable replacement, he'd give her a generous last check and send her on down the road.

His decision made, he moved to the side of the truck. Grabbing the last of the boxes, he leaned into the truck bed beside her.

She turned to him and smiled. "Are we ready to go home?"

C heap, damn sunglasses! Even with her shades on the blazing sunshine made her squint. Following as close as she could behind the ancient Ford pickup, she was still afraid she'd lose Micah in the curves, hills and dust. "What did you get yourself into this time, Crockett?"

Dirty tan clouds of powdery sand billowed from beneath Micah West's truck's tires and filtered through her open window. Dust coated her hair and jeans a pale brown, her mouth tasted like she'd eaten dirt and her eyes—her eyes were screaming.

She'd love to roll up her window and turn on the air, but neither had worked for at least three hundred miles. For the umpteenth time in the last few hours, she second-guessed her decision to hire on with the cowboy, but she knew becoming a camp cook in the high desert was her best alternative. No one from her former life would think of looking for her here.

Pansy had loaned her the dark green Ford Focus, but even Pansy didn't know where she'd gone.

When she had enough money to move back East and start over, she'd quit this end-of-the-road job. Out of her limited number of choices, this was the one most likely to keep her safe—to keep her alive.

She'd asked a few questions before they started for the ranch, trying to get a feel for her new employer. She'd tried to make small talk, but all she got was one-word answers and sometimes only a grunt. Micah might be uncommunicative, but weighing his reticence against Mad Dog's malevolence, she'd take silence every time.

After a few miles on the wash-boarded road surrounded by barren landscape, she was ready to turn back. She could head west and get lost in Portland or make her way to Canada. She'd always wanted to see Canada. Except she didn't have a passport, and she had less than thirty dollars in her wallet. She hadn't dared to go to the bank before she left for fear Mad Dog was watching her.

And it wasn't as if she had much money left. After Ken had helped himself to most of her savings, running into Mad Dog again wasn't worth the risk. Paranoid maybe, but the cigarette burn was still raw, and she couldn't bear to think of what he'd do next time.

She focused her gaze on the passing countryside and turned her thoughts away from her troubles. The landscape was beautiful in a stark kind of way—no cars or stores, no people. Or very few and the ones she'd met weren't exactly the friendly types.

"Umpphhh!" Her butt repeatedly bounced against the worn seat again as Pansy's little car climbed gracelessly over the ruts. She considered honking to get Micah's attention, maybe suggest a break, but the horn didn't work either. When she'd about given up, he slowed and turned left onto a one-lane path. Wagon track was a better description.

Micah parked in the middle of the road and walked back. He squatted beside the car, his hands on his thighs. "Almost there." He glanced at her for a split second then returned his gaze to the countryside.

Black hair curled over the collar of his shirt. Over six feet tall, with muscular shoulders, a narrow waist and long, denim-clad legs, he presented a picture of masculine grace. In the few seconds he'd looked at her before shifting his gaze, she was mesmerized. His eyes were the color of the summer sky, deep and clear. He was rough and ranch, like the rawhide her grandfather used to braid.

Ah, Gramps. He'd been her one source of stability in a childhood filled with change, and he'd been dead for more years than she wanted to count. The mere thought of him brought back the bitter taste of little squares of black licorice he'd carve up with his pocketknife and the sweet scent of his pipe tobacco.

"Almost there, but the road gets rough." He put one hand on the window and stood.

"You said it wasn't far when we left town. I'm not sure I believe you." She smiled. He had to be joking. The road ahead was worse than the one they'd been on?

"Your choice." His words were sharp and short without a speck of fun.

Seriously, did this man not have a humorous bone in his body? She reached out and touched his forearm. The muscles moved beneath her hand as he stiffened. Warmth flowed through her fingers straight to her heart. "I was kidding."

"The ranch house is over the next hill." His gaze dropped. He looked at her hand on his arm then raised his electric blue gaze. "What are you doing in this area?"

His abrupt change of subject caught her off guard. She'd

spent much of the drive devising answers to that question, but she couldn't think of a single one right now. She drew her hand away and scooted back into the car. "I'm, uh..." Great answer, Cary. She spit out the first thing that came to mind. "I'm going on a quest."

Go figure. That got a laugh. His face transformed from angry and cold to warm and beautiful in the second it took for him to smile.

"A quest?" He kept his smile and attention on her, throwing off sparks of attraction. "What is a quest?"

She could answer this question. Her ex-boyfriend, the thief, had talked about going on his quest to find ancient gold coins. He'd never made any effort to save the money needed or worked to find a site. He'd just talked. "You know, a mission, a pursuit of the heart." It sounded no more rational coming from her mouth than it had from Ken's but it was better than sitting here mute.

"Your pursuit of the heart is finding sagebrush in eastern Oregon?" He shook his head, the smile gone. "You need to get out more."

She turned back to the hillsides filled with sage and cheat grass. He was making fun of her, but at least he'd spoken. "My quest is to see the United States."

Her first quest was to not get killed, but he didn't need to know that.

THE APRIL AFTERNOON was unseasonably warm, and Micah rolled his sleeves up to his elbows. Talking to Cary left him unsettled. He was both attracted to the blonde and uneasy in her presence. She wasn't telling him the whole truth, but that was okay. She wouldn't be here long enough to make any difference. A week or two of cooking and he'd have found someone else. Someone more qualified to do the work.

Someone who was a man.

He placed his palm on the top of her rattletrap of a car and leaned down to glance inside. "Follow me." With only a mile to go, she shouldn't have much trouble, but the little green car she was driving wouldn't make the trip many more times.

As they topped the last rise, the ranch came into view. A smile warred with his normally taciturn expression. His great-grandfather founded the Circle W. The land had been in the family for over one hundred years.

He pulled up to the back of the ranch house and turned off the key. No matter how many times he looked at the old house, he never lost the surge of pride that it was his. White clapboard siding and tall double-hung windows, gave off a warm vibe. This was his home, and he loved it with all his heart.

By the time he climbed out and rounded the back of the truck, Cary stood beside her car, looking at the house.

"It's . . . this is . . . oh wow . . . beautiful." As she turned, he noticed her eyes had filled with tears, but she turned away and walked around the side of the house. "Is it okay if I look around?"

"I got work to do. Help yourself." He knew he was being abrupt, but the fact that she was here at all disturbed him.

She whirled around and started back. "Sorry. I forgot about the groceries." Climbing onto the tire, she reached into the back of the truck. Filling her arms with as many bags as she could carry, she smiled at him as she started up the walk.

Micah hefted two large boxes of supplies and led the way into the house. "Come on."

Placing the bags on the counter, Cary twirled in a circle. "This is amazing. I've always wanted an old house to remodel." Her smile was wide and her eyes shining.

The kitchen must look worn and dated to the city girl, and that was too damned bad. "Not good enough for you. I figured as much." He dropped the boxes on the counter and strode out the back door. He should have figured a prissy city girl would find fault. Like Marlene, nothing out here would be good enough for her.

As he reached into the truck bed for another box, he felt a soft touch on his shoulder. When he turned, her golden eyes gazed at him. "I didn't mean that. I love the house."

"My family has lived on this land since 1885. My great-great-grandfather built this house in 1910." He pointed to the square clapboard building south of the barn. The original whitewashed siding had faded to a soft gray and patches of moss grew on the roof, but the red brick chimney stood straight and proud. "That's the original home."

She stared at the smaller building then turned to him. "I can't imagine having roots like this. My family never stayed anywhere long enough to build anything."

Micah couldn't imagine not having the ranch, not belonging to the land. He almost reached out to Cary and pulled her to him, but that would never do. He stuffed his hands into his back pockets.

"Can I look inside?" She raised a hand, pointing to the little house.

With a short nod, Micah led the way across the barnyard. He placed the toe of his boot against the bottom of the door. As he twisted the doorknob, he lifted and pushed. With a squeal of wood against wood, the door gave.

He stepped back to allow Cary access to the one-room shack.

She entered and walked to the middle of the room. "Over one hundred years old and I could live in here." She lifted the multi-colored quilt, log cabin squares whirling across the fabric, from the back of the old wooden rocker and shook it out. "Who made this?"

Micah leaned against the dry sink. "Grams." He remembered her sitting at her old Singer, piecing the red, blue and green squares when he'd been no more than five. "She loved to sew."

Cary carefully refolded it then placed it back on the chair. "I can't sew worth beans. Good thing I can cook." Her head whipped around, her expression determined. "I can cook, you know."

"I didn't say you couldn't." He just thought she couldn't cook for the ranch hands. She wasn't a man. She wasn't even a cowgirl. "Come on back to the house. When we have the groceries put away, I'll show you the bunkhouse and introduce you to some of the men."

They hadn't made it halfway across the barnyard when a tiny, redheaded whirlwind raced out the barn door and leaped into his arms.

"Hey, Willa Wild. Where you been?" Little arms wrapped around his neck, and he felt a sloppy kiss on his cheek.

"Me and Toby been feeding the baby calves, Pa." The sight of his eight year old daughter made his world right again. He felt her body tense as her head turned. "Who's she?"

Micah raised his gaze to meet Cary's eyes and thought he saw a flash of sadness there. When he stopped to study her, it was gone and a bright smile transformed her face. He set his daughter on her feet. "This is Cary. She's going to cook for the hands . . . and us."

Cary held out her hand, her expression solemn. "Nice to meet you, Willa."

"My name's Willa Wild." Her big blue eyes shifted to her father then she moved her gaze back to Cary. Her grubby hand darted out and grabbed Cary's manicured one.

"Willa Wild? What a pretty name. I don't think I've ever heard it before."

"That's because I'm one of a kind. Right, Pa?"

"Right." He watched the platinum blonde shake hands with his daughter. He determined to keep Cary at arm's length. His little girl didn't need another disappointment in her young life.

Willa Wild grabbed his hand and tugged him toward the barn. "Come on, Pa. Let's show Cary the new calves."

At the far end of the barn, in a small pen, stood two black calves barely bigger than large dogs. Cary dropped to her knees and reached out to pet one. When the calf latched onto her finger and sucked, Cary fell back onto her butt. Her soft shriek caused the calf to jump and back away a step.

Willa Wild laughed. "It's okay. They think you have something for them to eat." She stuck her small fingers through the fence, and the calf made loud slurping noises as it nuzzled her hand. "See."

Cary crawled closer and studied the girl and the calf. Willa Wild pulled her hand away and walked to the shelf beside the pen. She picked up a large white bottle with a red nipple. "We feed them morning and night."

Cary looked at him. "Where are their mothers?" She slowly lowered her hand into the pen, allowing the calf to suck. Her soft voice did strange things to Micah's chest.

Micah cleared his throat and tried to clear his head.

"The little heifer is a twin, and the cow didn't have enough milk. The other one—"

"Black Bart. Me and Toby named him today."

Micah's heart stuttered as Willa turned her tiny face to him. She looked so much like her mother. Thank heavens she got her personality from Gram. The only thing his ex-wife had done right was to leave Willa Wild here on the ranch. "Black Bart it is. What did you name the other one?"

Willa Wild jumped up and pointed across the fence. "She's Lil' Bit, 'cause she is." She looked at Cary. "Want to see my pig?"

Prior to arriving in East Hope, if anyone had suggested Cary would be at home on a ranch, she'd have laughed until she cried. Her idea of a good time had always been a nice dinner out and a movie or concert. She hadn't had a one-on-one relationship with dirt since she was six. Her mother hadn't allowed it.

Cary looked at the slime on her hand then shrugged and wiped it on her jeans.

If this little pixie wasn't fazed by calf slobber, neither was she. She smiled at the little girl and took her hand. The closest she'd ever been to a pig was bacon. Now was as good a time as any to see where her favorite breakfast food came from.

They wove their way behind the barn, through bent, rusted metal panels and rolls of barbed wire. In the corner, beneath an old cottonwood tree was a ramshackle pen made from pallets tied together with thin orange rope.

Willa Wild climbed over the wooden fence and stuck her fingers in her mouth. A high-pitched whistle rocketed through the air.

Forceful snorting made Cary take one step back and then another when a huge beast raised itself out of a pile of straw in the corner of the pen. "What is that smell?"

"Come here, Tinkerbelle." The miniscule child climbed on the pig's back and rode her around the pen. She laid full length on Tinkerbelle and wrapped her arms as far as they'd go around the hog's middle. "She doesn't smell so good, but she's as smart as a dog."

Cary stepped forward again, breathing through her mouth and looked at the sparse, wiry hair that covered the Pepto-Bismol pink pig. "I've never been this close to a pig. I'm not sure I want to be this close again. Why is it you want a pig instead of a dog?"

Willa Wild's face crinkled into a grin. "Last year, we bought Tinkerbell for my 4H project." The grin slid into a frown. "You tell her, Pa."

Micah rubbed his hand over his face. "Willa Wild raised Tinkerbell from a piglet and took her to the fair. She won a blue ribbon. At the end of the fair, they auction the 4H project animals."

"They were going to kill her." Willa Wild's voice rose to an even higher pitch, but when the pig grew restless, she lowered it to a whisper. "But Pa didn't let them."

"I should say not." Cary turned to Micah, her hands on her hips. "You mean all these children have to sell their pets for slaughter?" What had she gotten herself into? Civilized people didn't treat kids or animals this way.

"They aren't pets, they're livestock." He looked down his nose at her before turning toward the house. "Come on, Willa Wild. We've got work to do."

Cary watched as the tall dark rancher took the hand of the little redheaded sprite and walked away. She was so far out of her element she couldn't even see the fence. If she had any choice, she'd leave right this minute and not look back. But she didn't have a choice. Not if she wanted to keep away from the burning end of Mad Dog's punishment.

As she walked back to the house, the scent of roses and hay floated along on a light breeze. It was a refreshing change from Eau de Pig. She stopped and tipped her head up, marveling at the deep blue dome above. Where she'd come from, smog from the over-concentration of motor vehicles colored the sky an off shade of gray even on clear spring days.

She hurried to the house and climbed the steps, wishing she'd been raised like Micah, with a family and the sure knowledge he belonged. But no matter how hard she wished it, facts didn't change. She was alone, and she'd come to terms with that.

The grocery bags were right where she'd left them, and she busied herself finding where the food went.

It was four o'clock by the time she'd familiarized herself with the layout. Micah hadn't said she'd be responsible for dinner tonight, so when she found her bags in a small room upstairs, she put things away.

"Hullo." A deep voice carried to her bedroom.

Cary hurried down to find the man who'd been with Micah in town standing in the middle of the kitchen. Well-worn Wranglers, a faded red plaid shirt and scuffed boots gave Cary her first clues that this was either a neighbor or a ranch hand.

"Hi," Cary said. "Micah isn't here. Can I help you?" Hopefully, he wouldn't ask her to help because she barely knew the way to the barn. Maybe he was just lost, and she could point him the way to town.

"Course he isn't. It's feedin' time." He walked over,

opened the door of the oven and peered inside before letting the door slam shut. "Nobody started dinner yet. The crew is gonna be mighty hungry. Can you cook?"

Dinner? Micah had left her here with no idea of what he expected of her. He'd said seven hands. Did he mean himself and Willa Wild, too? "I'm sorry. I didn't catch your name."

He stepped forward and held out his hand. "Barnes, Clinton Barnes." His fingers were tobacco stained and rough. It seemed people out here were big on shaking hands. Even Willa Wild had offered hers.

"I'm Cary Calhoun, and I can cook."

"Better hurry. The men are driving in right now." He pointed to the window and sure enough, here came a group of cowboys.

Cary racked her brain. What could she make in a few minutes? Only one thing came to mind. She hurried to the refrigerator and pulled out two-dozen eggs. The heavy cast iron skillet heated on the gas stove. She found a large package of sausage and crumbled it into the pan. At least this wasn't part of Willa Wild's pet pig. Besides, she didn't have time to question animal morality right now.

She whipped up a dozen eggs at a time, added chopped tomatoes, onions and cheese and started the first of many omelets.

As the men filed into the kitchen, a loud catcall sounded through the room. "Hey, honey. What's a cute little thing like you doing here?"

On the streets of home, she'd have had a caustic comeback to the condescending comment, but she bit her tongue and forced a smile that she hoped said she was glad to be here. She needed this job. "Cooking dinner."

"Well, you're a little late. We're here." The sweat-soaked band of the gray cowboy hat the young man wore looked like it was older than he was, but his smile seemed genuine.

"Sorry. It's my first day on the job." She looked from face to face, but the only friendly one was the young man with the hat. "I'll have something in just a minute." She placed the first omelet on a plate, added a sprig of parsley she'd grabbed at the grocery store, and put the plate in front of the closest cowboy. Whirling back to the stove, she poured another measure of eggs into the pan.

"Where's mine?" A rough voice broke her concentration.

"Eggs? Eggs are for breakfast." Another man spoke.

She looked over her shoulder at the seven men. "Just a minute." It was a struggle to keep the panic out of her voice.

"We don't have a minute. We're hungry." One of the men thumped his fists against the top of the table. Another rose and came to stand behind her. "Is this all you're making for dinner? Cause I could eat all of that myself."

Cary's mind clouded and her hands shook. She needed this job, and if the hands didn't like what she cooked, Micah would let her go. She hadn't even been here long enough to earn gas money. "This is just the appetizer. Sit back down and have a beer while I cook."

She opened the refrigerator and handed out cold bottles of beer. Mr. Barnes shook his head. "Don't drink," He stood and walked out the back door.

"Don't mind him. He's always grouchy." The youngest had placed his hat on the floor and held up his hand. "I got dibs on the next plate of food."

COULD this week get any worse? First Cookey quits then the banker gets all-uppity, and now Micah had a really bad feeling about Cary, the replacement cook. Hiring a young woman to work with these men was just wrong, but he hadn't had a choice.

Enough of the bad vibes. No use calling trouble by name. He might as well go in and check on dinner. She probably had everything under control. How hard could it be to cook a simple dinner for the men? Women knew how to cook. His grandpa always said it was in their genes.

The sound of angry voices overlaid with laughter and a lone woman's voice reached him before he opened the back door. Shit, shit, shit!

He turned the knob and pushed the door just as a plate of something hit the wall beside his head. The scene was chaotic. Smoke billowed out of a pan on the stove. Two of the men were on their feet with Cary in the middle. She had a hand on the chests of two men, trying to push them apart.

He slammed the door to get everyone's attention. "What the hell is going on?"

The noisy room filled with silence, and the tension was as thick as a good steak. Cary's eyes were wide and her lips quivered. "Nothing. Just a little misunderstanding." She took the larger cowboy's hand and led him to the table. "Byron, please sit down." After a scorching look at the other man, he did as she asked.

Micah watched as she moved to Tim, the newest employee and did the same only on the other side of the table.

She turned to Micah. "This is all my fault. I'm late with dinner and the men are hungry. Don't be mad at them." Then she moved to the smoking pan on the stove, dumped whatever burned thing was inside into the sink and placed it back on the burner. "I'll have something in just a minute."

Her voice sounded calm, but Micah saw her swipe at her eyes with her left hand. He swept his gaze around the room then pulled out his wallet and handed a hundred-dollar bill to Barnes as he walked back into the kitchen. "Take the men into town and buy them dinner."

Cary whirled around, her dark eyes huge in her elfin face. "No. I can cook."

Micah waved to the men and waited until they'd all left the room before turning back to Cary.

"I can do this. Don't fire me." She twisted her hands as she walked toward him.

"Got any coffee?"

"What? Yes." She grabbed a cup from the counter, filled it and placed it on the table in front of him. Then she stepped back and waited.

"You want one?" When she shook her head, he pointed to the chair at the end of the oak table. "Sit down. Please."

Her shoulders slumped, and he could almost hear the defeat coming off her. He was going to regret this. Hell, he already regretted it. "I'm not going to fire you."

She raised her head, disbelief in her eyes.

"This is my fault. I didn't make it clear that you needed to cook tonight." He took a sip of the coffee then stared into the cup as if the liquid could tell him why it was so good. "This is great."

Cary's sigh was so big it almost lifted her from the chair. "Fresh ground Tanzanian Peaberry. I brought it from home."

He looked at the dark liquid again. How could something with a name like that be good? He took another sip.

"You're not firing me?" Cary's expectant expression tugged at his heart. She leaned against the back of the chair then ran a hand through the longer hair over her eyes.

"No. Not tonight." Her gaze jerked up to his and her lips opened into a soft pink O. "I still don't think this will work, but tonight wasn't your fault." The sound of his daughter's voice stopped that thought.

"Pa, can I go to town with Barnsey?" She ran to him and jumped into his lap. Placing her hands on his cheeks like she did when she wanted something, she gave him a kiss. "Can I? Please?"

Clinton Barnes stood in the doorway his fingers stuffed into the front pockets of his Wranglers. "Okay by me," he said when Micah looked at him. "I'll bring her back as soon as we're done eating."

Micah shifted his gaze from his daughter to the foreman then back. "Okay, but you mind your manners. I'll know if you eat like a monkey."

Willa Wild wrapped her skinny arms around his neck and gave him one of her wonderful hugs. "Thanks, Pa." She was off his lap in an instant, running for the door, her knobby knees and skinny legs wobbling like a new colt's. She grabbed Clinton's hand and tugged. "Come on, Barnsey. They'll eat all the French fries before we get there."

"You eat something besides French fries." Micah knew as he said the words neither of them would listen.

"We wouldn't think of it, would we Willa Wild?" The old man laughed as he followed the little girl outside.

Micah turned back to Cary. "Well, I guess it's just you and me. What's for dinner?"

Cary stared at him for a short minute then turned to the stove. "Eggs."

He fought the smile that tugged at his lips. "I'm allergic to eggs."

Her shoulders lifted almost to her ears. She pulled in a deep breath, and he watched her ribcage move with the effort. When she turned, her face was grim, but she moved to the refrigerator and opened the door.

"I can make tuna sandwiches, toasted, or tomato soup." She turned slowly and looked at him. One tear spilled from her eye and she wiped it away quickly. "Or both."

Micah rose and crossed the room, pushing the refrigerator door shut. He put his hands on her shoulders and moved her to the table. The desire to pull her into his arms and comfort her was strong, but he'd given in to that urge before and look where that had gotten him. "Sit down. I'll cook." He pulled a Kleenex from the box and handed it to her. "And I was kidding about the eggs. Sorry, I'm not very funny."

Cary walked to the window and stared out while she blew her nose. "It's okay. The way my week has gone, it seemed like an allergy to eggs would be par for the course."

Liquor bottles filled the end cupboard. Micah pulled out a bottle of whiskey. With two glasses and a bottle of 7-Up, he mixed each of them a drink. He took a sip, nodded and set one glass in front of Cary. "This will make things better."

He whipped up eggs and poured them into the pan. As they cooked, he chopped a jalapeno pepper, olives and an onion, adding them to the eggs. Adding a pile of grated cheese, he flipped the omelet then grabbed a glass jar from the refrigerator.

"My grandmother made the salsa. It's the last jar we have left." He slid the giant omelet onto a plate and cut half off for Cary. "Try this."

As Micah hunkered down over the dinner, Cary picked at hers. She looked up and watched him.

He felt her gaze settle on him and raised his eyes to hers. "What?"

"How long since your grandmother passed?" She turned her attention back to the eggs. "Never mind. Not my business."

"I don't mind. Grams and Pops raised me from the time I was five. She was the most important person in my life until Willa Wild came along. Grams died ten years ago, Pops last year." The thought of his kind, loving grandma made him feel better, and he relaxed. Unlike Pops, she'd always loved him just as he was.

"You're lucky to have someone in your life like that." Cary cut off a big bite of omelet and chewed. "This is good. Really good!" She dipped the spoon into the salsa and added more to her dinner.

"Be careful with that stuff. The heat sneaks up on you." Just as the words came out of his mouth, her eyes widened and a pink flush worked up her neck to her cheeks.

She flapped her hand in front of her mouth as if that would temper the heat. "Wa! Wa! Water!" She grabbed her glass and chugged the rest of the whiskey then ran to the sink and put her head beneath the faucet and drank. When she'd had enough, she stood, wiping her mouth with the back of her hand. "Sneaks up on you is an understatement."

If she'd been one of his friends, he'd be on the floor laughing. But he contained his mirth and handed her a towel. "You'll get used to it."

"I don't know if I want to get used to it. Maybe I'll stick to this." Cary scraped the excess salsa off her omelet and added a spoonful of sour cream.

Micah opened the pantry door and pulled out a package of cookies. "We can have Oreos for dessert if you'll promise not to tell Willa Wild."

Her city-girl smile set his heart to dancing, but he pulled it up short. The attraction he felt for Cary was dangerous. She was passing through, and there was no way he was getting involved. Time to end the friendly chat and get back to business. He put the package in front of her. "I've got things to do. Put the cookies in the top of the pantry when you're done."

## 4

W aking at five a.m. wasn't a hardship for Cary. She'd worked the morning shift at Chez Romeo for two years, arriving at work by four a.m. to bake delectable breakfast goodies for an increasing crowd. It was a little harder this morning. She'd spent the majority of the night thinking of the quick change in attitude Micah had pulled last night.

Baking had always been her escape, and she needed to escape thoughts of her new boss. She searched through cupboard doors until she found a large bowl. The least she could do was to make cranberry croissants for breakfast.

What had happened last night? All the while Micah worked on dinner and during the meal, he'd been friendly, interested in what she had to say. Cary thought they were getting to know each other. Then he pulled out a package of cookies, looked at her like she'd grown an extra head and hurried out in a huff.

Strange didn't begin to describe Micah West. Strange and bone-melting hot.

She sifted flour into the bowl, adding sugar, baking

powder and orange zest. As she cut in the butter, she thought of how he'd acted. Micah had walked into the pantry, a welcome-to-my-world smile on his face and walked out looking like Mars, the Roman god of anger. No matter how many times she ran through their interaction, it didn't make any sense.

Her arm muscles strained as she mixed cream and eggs into the batter. There was probably a mixer around here somewhere, but she was used to baking by hand. She'd been so frightened of Mad Dog finding out she was running, she hadn't dared to take any of her utensils. To be a great cook, she needed great tools, and she'd saved for each top of the line spatula, turner and strainer. Hopefully Pansy would think to get them before her landlord threw them out.

Good thing she'd found the bag of dried cranberries at the grocery yesterday. She folded the fruit into the scone batter then dumped the dough onto a section of countertop she'd floured. Kneading it helped work off some of the tension remaining from the sleepless night.

Cary rolled the dough into a circle and cut wedges. Slipping the scones into the oven, she poured her third cup of coffee this morning and sat at the table for a few minutes of relaxation. Scones, coffee and orange juice would be a great way to feed the cowboys. She'd screwed up last night, but she'd make up for it this morning.

She was slicing a cantaloupe and adding the pieces to a bowl of fresh fruit when Clinton Barnes walked in the door.

He took off his John Deere gimme cap and hung it on the hook by the door. "Hello, Miss Cary. What's for breakfast?" The grizzled cowboy selected a cup from the dozen sitting on the counter and poured himself a cup of coffee.

Cary smiled as she brought the heaping platter of scones

to the table. "A treat." She grabbed the huge bowl of fruit and set it in front of the man. "Here you go."

Barnes looked from the food to Cary's face and back again. He took one of the scones and took a bite. Licking his lips, he grinned. "These are good. What else have you got?"

"Uh..." She turned in a circle as if by magic something would appear to answer his question. She dropped into a chair across the scarred table from Barnes and dropped her face into her hands. "I've been up since five baking these. Aren't they enough?"

Barnes dropped the scone and reached out to tap her hand. When she looked up, he grinned. He was younger than she'd first thought, maybe late forties. "These are real good, but the men need real food. They work hard and need protein." He took another bite and sighed.

"I have eggs." Cary dropped her head and bounced her forehead against the table. "God, all I seem to have to cook is eggs."

"Eggs are a start. You don't have long, but you have time to whip up a big batch of scrambled eggs and some bacon." Barnes finished off his scone and reached for another one. "These will work great to finish off their breakfast."

Cary scrambled two-dozen eggs, adding chopped onion and peppers. As they cooked, she made a mound of toast and fried two pounds of bacon. She could hear the men outside the door as she placed the breakfast on the table. With a forced smile, she moved on to the back porch to let them eat.

Micah had let her off last night, but if he found out how she'd tried to feed his crew, especially after his mood swing, he'd kiss her ass good-bye without the kiss. She lowered herself to the top step on the back porch. For a woman who'd taken care of herself since she was seventeen, she was mucking up this job. The sound of a pair of heavy boots hitting the boards of the porch caught her attention.

Mr. Barnes sat beside her and handed her a cup of coffee. "I love the high desert in the morning."

She hadn't had time to look at the desert or anything else around here, and the way things were going, she wouldn't. Past the irrigated fields, the sagebrush filled valley gave way to Juniper covered hills. The sweet scent of grass, sage and pine calmed her nerves. In the far distance, tall snow-capped mountains caught her eye. She pointed at them with her cup. "They're beautiful."

Barnes took a sip of his coffee. "The Three Sisters. The north sister is Faith, the middle, Hope and the youngest and tallest is Charity." He turned his gaze from the scenery to Cary.

Cary tried to smile, to convince the man she had every-thing under control. She swallowed down the lump in her throat. Who was she kidding? She was as far from being in control as a kitten at a dog show. "Can I tell you something?"

He looked back to the mountain and nodded, giving her time.

"I can't cook." Words rushed out of her mouth like a raging river. "I mean I can, but I bake. I'm a pastry chef."

"I know."

She wrapped her arms around her waist, fighting to control her emotions. How much could she tell this man? "I've never cooked for this many men."

"I know that, too," Barnes said then took another sip and stared at the scenery. "Look in the cupboard above the fridge and pull out the little wooden box with the rooster painted on the front. That's Minerva's recipe box."

"Minerva?" Cary picked up her cup.

Barnes stood and walked out into the sparse backyard.

He turned to Cary. "Minerva was Micah's grandmother. Fine woman and no better cook anywhere on this earth. You check that out." He handed Cary his cup and disappeared around the corner of the house. She heard a diesel engine start and watched the plume of dust as her first friend in East Hope drove away. He hadn't said many words, but he'd given her a wonderful present—hope.

She hurried back into the kitchen and chatted with the men as they tied their silk scarves in fancy knots, slipped into their coats and pulled on their boots. As they filed out the door, she called, "See you at lunch."

She got by with sandwiches and soup for lunch, and since it was Saturday, she didn't have to cook dinner.

By the time evening arrived, Willa Wild had gone to the neighbors to play with their kids, and she hadn't seen Micah all day. After cleaning the kitchen, she finally got time to look for the recipes. She sat at the table, ran her hand over the smooth wood and slowly lifted the lid.

Four by six inch white cards, covered with flowery writing, filled the recipe box. Along with the alphabetical dividers, there were several more handwritten in delicate scrolled letters. Micah's grandmother had arranged complete meals for breakfast, lunch, and dinner.

Cary pulled out the breakfast cards and shuffled through them. There were at least ten different recipes and all were scaled to feed ten hungry men.

She was trying to fit them back into the box when Micah entered from the living room. She looked up and smiled. "Hey, look what I found."

He didn't smile back. In fact, his expression filled with thunder. "Get your hands off that!"

∼

THE RECIPE BOX was one of only a few things Micah had left of his grandmother. By the time he'd gotten home from college for her funeral, his grandfather had cleaned and boxed up everything of hers and given it away. Micah knew it was grief that caused the reaction, but it didn't make things better. The old man must have forgotten about the box.

"I didn't mean to bite your head off." He took the cards from Cary's hands and straightened them before replacing them. "Grams kept all her favorite recipes in here. I need to make copies if you're going to use them."

He turned and walked across the room to the window, but he didn't see the view. The sight of the box brought Grams to the front of his thoughts.

Willa Wild flew through the door and skidded to a stop. "What's up, Pa?" Dirt streaked her small face, and she held a squirming, red puppy under one arm. "See what Mrs. Turner gave me."

He looked at the fat mongrel in her arms. *God save me from the good intentions of my neighbors.* "Willa, you know we talked about this. No more dogs."

His beautiful little daughter melted into a puddle of misery on the floor, but he wasn't giving in this time. This is the way they got dogs three and four. "Willa Wild, enough."

She looked up, her tear-streaked face pinched in a great imitation of Scarlett O'Hara. "But he'll die if I don't take care of him, and Mrs. Turner said she wouldn't take him back." She turned to Cary. "Do you want a dog? He's a good one."

Micah bent down and touched Willa's shoulder. "Cary doesn't want the puppy. Take him back to Mrs. Turner." He lifted his daughter off the floor and put her on her feet. The puppy waddled over to Cary and wiggled in front of her in a fit of puppy joy. He watched as she bent and scratched him behind the ears.

"His name is Goodun." Willa grinned. "Because he is."

"Goodun?" Cary picked up the pup and rubbed his ears.

"You know. Good one." Willa Wild hurried over to Cary. "I thought he was meant to be mine, but I can see he's yours."

Cary tried to hand the pup back to the girl. "I don't think—"

Time to stop this foolishness. "Willa Wild, take the puppy home. Cary doesn't want a dog. She doesn't have a place to keep it." He looked up expecting the woman to be grateful he'd solved the problem, only to be scorched by the angry look on her face.

"You seem to be superb at assuming things, Mr. West." Cary picked up the puppy and started toward the door. She stopped by Willa and touched her shoulder. "I think you're right. Goodun and I will be great friends."

His gaze got caught on her jeans-clad legs and the enticing way her rear end swayed as she moved up the stairs. A tug on his sleeve brought his attention back to his daughter. Except for the missing front teeth, her wide smile reminded him of his ex-wife. She would be a beauty one of these days. She was a handful at eight. What was it going to be like when she started dating? "We discussed this. You promised no more dogs."

"But, Pa. She had a gunny sack. She said she'd throw him in the river." Her lip quivered, and she worked to squeeze a tear out of her eye.

"You know that isn't true. Mrs. Turner wouldn't do that." He watched as she closed her eyes.

After a moment, her face relaxed, and she opened her baby blues. "Yes, but Pa, Mrs. Turner was going to take him to the pound, and Jimmy Martin says they kill the dogs there. I couldn't let him die." She drew in a shuddery breath. "I couldn't."

"Willa—"

The wide smile was back. "But this worked out just great, Pa. Goodun will keep Cary company so she won't be lonely."

His daughter could give Vivien Leigh a run for her money when it came to acting, and she hadn't even hit her teens yet. He put his arm around her thin shoulders. "Come on, Willa. Let's have one of these donuts with some ice cream."

When they'd finished their dessert, Willa gave him a kiss and ran upstairs to get cleaned up for bed. She kept his life entertaining to say the least. Thinking about his marriage still gave him heartburn, but having Willa in his life was worth every heartbreaking minute.

As he stacked the bowls in the sink, he heard a puppy's whine. Turning, he watched as the pup ran into the room, barked at him then squatted on the floor. A puddle spread from beneath the animal. He looked up to see Cary's horrified face.

"I'm so sorry. I didn't catch him quick enough." She lifted the pup and hurried toward the door.

Micah followed her outside and watched as she put the animal on the lawn. The faint moonlight glowed in the white strands of her hair. When she turned to him, his breath stuck in his throat and his heart raced.

"I've never had a pet before. Will you help me train Goodun?" Her smile faded away and her brow wrinkled. "I forgot. You were going to fire me before Willa came in with the puppy."

This was his chance. All he had to do was say yes, and

this crazy woman would pack her bag and leave. She'd probably even take the pup. He moved down the steps to stand in front of her. Opening his mouth to tell her she was right, the wrong words came out. "You seem to be superb at assuming things, Ms. Crockett." Where the hell had that come from?

Cary's smile lit up the dull night. She threw her arms around his neck and gave him a hug. Leaning back, her arms still around his neck, she said, "Thank you."

Micah moved without thinking. His hands settled on her hips, and he pulled her body against his. The feel of her soft lips against his made him forget everything he needed to remember. Time slowed, and he got lost in her scent and feel, falling deeper with each passing second. He might have kissed Cary all night if Willa hadn't chosen that moment to reappear.

"Pa, aren't you going to tuck me in?" The voice came from the back door.

Startled, Micah jumped back. He heard the soft exclamation of dismay from Cary. "Go pick out a book, and I'll be up in a minute." The screen door slammed, and he took a moment to gather his thoughts. He almost took a moment too long.

Cary hurried toward the corner of the house.

"Where are you going?" Micah hurried after her, grabbing her hand and pulling her back to him.

"I can't do that." Cary kept her gaze on the ground and tugged at the hold he had on her hand.

"My fault." Micah let go of her hand but stepped in front of her. "Won't happen again." He hoped he sounded sincere, because he wasn't sure he could keep the promise.

"Damn right it won't."

## 5

C ary lengthened her stride as she hurried toward barn, not quite running, looking over her shoulder every few steps to make sure Micah hadn't followed. Only a few orange rays remained from the setting sun, casting long shadows across the packed dirt. When she slid the heavy barn door shut, darkness engulfed her.

Running her hands along the rough boards beside the door, she felt the smooth plastic of the light switch. As she flipped the switch, a dim bulb high in the rafters gave her enough light to make her way along the aisle. When she reached the pen with the baby calves, she dropped to the straw-strewn floor. What was she thinking?

When Micah had kissed her, she didn't think. Her brain short-circuited, and her body mutinied. She'd felt an attraction to the cowboy since the moment she'd spotted him in the café, and she'd worked to control it. But the moment his lips had touched hers tonight, her hard-fought-for control had disappeared into a poof of lust.

She didn't need a man in her life. Her time with Ken

proved she had lousy taste in men, and she wasn't sure she could survive another heartbreak. But that was the least of her worries.

She was sure she couldn't survive the fear she'd lived with after Ken left her to face Mad Dog alone. A shiver of dread raced across her skin, raising goose bumps all along her arms. Cary jumped to her feet. She drew in a long breath and held it until her heart rate slowed. There were no bad guys here. The calves weren't worried. They were curled into black balls in the straw.

*Get your act together, Crockett.* Mad Dog wouldn't find her here. Not yet. Patsy had promised to call if she noticed anything unusual.

A few more weeks here, just until she'd saved enough to make her escape, and she'd disappear once more. Everyone would be happy.

Walking back to the house, Cary sucked in a calming breath with each step. She hesitated outside the front door then sank onto a porch chair. The setting sun cast a golden glow. Several Daffodils along the walk bloomed, and the buds on the lilac bushes swelled to bursting. She relaxed and let her thoughts turn to Micah. She didn't know him well, but she was sure he wouldn't force himself on her. All she had to do was make it clear she wasn't interested in him, or sex.

The thought of Micah naked and in her bed sent a scorching charge through her cells. The man was not at all what she usually went for, but someone had forgotten to tell her brain. Micah West was exactly what her body wanted.

In desperation, she turned her thoughts to Willa Wild.

Where was the little girl's mother, and who was she? Did Micah still have feelings for her? Willa would probably tell her if she asked, but it was better for everyone if she didn't get involved. As soon as she had enough money to leave the state, she'd be on her way to New York and the rest of her life.

With a glorious burst of color, the sun sank below the horizon, coloring the very air a magical pink. Shadows from the giant pine striped the grass and flowers. She took one last wistful glance around the yard and entered the house.

Closing the door, she turned just as Micah descended the stairs. Heat covered her throat and settled on her cheeks. Maybe he was as embarrassed as she was. If she ignored him . . .

"Have a nice visit with the calves?" Micah followed her into the kitchen and leaned against the counter. His nonchalance in the face of her overreaction to the kiss caused irritation to flash through her body. His smile made her grit her teeth.

Apparently he wasn't as affected as she was by their kiss. Maybe he was used to kissing strange women. With his blue eyes, tantalizing smile and powerful shoulders, he must have women falling all over him. She was just a fool who got sucked into his sphere. "The calves are sleeping. Did you get Willa Wild tucked in?" She reached into the cupboard. The yellow mixing bowl she found had to be from the forties.

"Tucked in tight." He rose and filled a cup with cold coffee from the pot and stuck it in the microwave. "What are you making?"

Cary measured out flour, baking powder, sugar and salt and mixed it with the whisk she'd found beneath the hand towels in the bottom drawer. The red painted handle was chipped and one of the wires was bent, but the thought of Micah's grandmother using this to bake for her grandson warmed her heart.

"Apple cake." The butter she'd set out earlier in the day

was softened. She pulled several Gala apples from the refrigerator. The well-used Sunbeam Mixmaster she'd found in the pantry still worked, and she used it to build the sweet, rich cake.

Cary spent a good part of her childhood learning everything she could about baking at the Hot Cakes Bakery. Her mother had gone from one charity to another all through Cary's childhood, always busy saving everyone but her daughter.

Helen, the owner of Hot Cakes, had taken the little girl in and kept her from being lonely. This apple cake was the first dessert Helen had taught her how to bake.

"You look like you know what you're doing."

Micah's voice pulled her from her reverie. "Yeah, I do. Do you like apples?" She cut off a large piece and handed it to Micah. After she poured the batter into a round cake pan, she sliced the apples into wedges and slid them into the batter in a pinwheel pattern.

"My grandmother made an apple cranberry pie that was great," he said. He looked up, a wistful smile on his face. "Would you be able to make one of those?"

Her gaze jerked up; her eyes blazed into his. "Only if you give me permission to look at her recipes." She paused as if measuring her words. "I wasn't stealing anything you know."

"I know." Micah looked up, his coffee cup held between his fingers. He shrugged then stood. "It's just that the box is nearly all I have left of her. Pops gave away everything else." Reaching over her head, he pulled the recipe box from the shelf and placed it in her hands. "Feel free to use anything."

She waited for him to move away, but instead, he put his hands on the counter on either side of her.

Cary clutched the recipe box, using it to keep him from getting closer. It didn't work. He leaned in, his breath warming her neck, his lips a soft feather against her skin. With every intention of telling him off, she raised her gaze to his face, his mouth. She sucked in as much of a breath as she could with her lungs on strike, lifted to her toes and brushed her lips across his.

With the last of her reserves, she lowered to her heels and tried to turn away.

Micah wrapped his arms around her and pulled her close. "Don't go." The first kiss had been soft and sweet. This time the heat from his mouth scorched her lips, fueling her passion. He ran his tongue along the seam of her lips, the wet slick feel draining away the rest of her reservations.

In the recesses of her non-functioning brain, a speck of rationality still existed. Cary pushed against Micah's chest then ducked beneath his arm. Her shaky legs carried her to the other side of the table. What the hell was going on? The attraction she felt for Micah overwhelmed her.

He leaned against the counter, his eyes still on her. His breathing was fast, almost as fast as hers, and his eyelids were half closed. His desire filled the room, so thick it surrounded her.

*Can't do this.* If she became involved with Micah, she might want to stay. Who was she kidding? She'd stay without a second thought.

A picture of Willa Wild popped into her mind and then Mad Dog's face. She couldn't risk the little girl getting mixed up in her problems. Micah could take care of himself, but Mad Dog wasn't averse to using a kid to get what he wanted.

"I can't do this." Cary put down the box and hurried toward the door. When she looked back, he hadn't moved. "I'm married."

MICAH WOKE before dawn and pulled on his jeans and work shirt. He'd acted like a horny seventeen-year-old boy last night, and he needed to apologize. The two kisses were burned into his memory and just thinking about Cary made him hard.

He needed to get his head together. He didn't have the time or inclination to play with a woman, much less a married one. Why had she waited so long to mention that little tidbit? Kind of a funny thing to keep a secret. And if she was married, why was she here? And where was her husband? Something didn't make sense with her latest revelation.

He hurried downstairs to make coffee and line out his day. Getting his mind back on ranching was the smart thing to do.

On a normal day, he was the first one up, brewing a pot of coffee. It took four minutes for the first cup to filter into the pot then he'd head for the office with the steaming mug.

As he descended the stairs, he noticed the pool of light shining through the kitchen door.

Some kind of steaming egg and potato casserole sat on the counter. Cary bent in front of the oven, positioning a second casserole dish and a huge pan of biscuits inside. The small, red pup slept on a towel by the door.

She stood, dropping the worn, handmade hot pads on the counter and then turned. Her hand flew to her chest as her eyes widened in surprise. "You scared the crap out of me. Next time make some noise."

At the sound of her voice, Goodun jumped to his feet. In a comical show of bravado, the pup ran in circles barking at whatever monster intended to harm his mistress.

A lock of white blonde hair curled over her forehead and her cheeks were flushed from the heat. She was beautiful in an offbeat, biker kind of way. No, she was beautiful in every way, and that was his problem. If anyone had asked him if he'd go for a woman like Cary, he'd have laughed. The only woman he'd become involved with that wasn't a cowgirl was Marlene and look how that had turned out.

Micah grabbed the cup of coffee from the microwave then pulled a chair up to the kitchen table. He took a sip, looking over the cup rim at her. "You're up early."

She bent down to reassure Goodun then returned to the stove. "I have breakfast to cook for your hands. I'd like to be ready today." She turned her back to him and started cutting up fruit. Neat squares of cantaloupe, watermelon and pineapple mixed with strawberries and blueberries. Micah recognized his grandmother's mixing bowl.

All thoughts of moving to his office vanished. His morning got better the longer he watched her move around the kitchen, her hips clad in well-fitting camouflage cargo pants, her army green T-shirt rising to give him tantalizing peeks of the creamy skin at her waist when she reached into the cupboards for ingredients.

He took another sip as she turned and found him watching her. Before he could react, she threw the washrag at his head, missing him by less than an inch. Hot coffee splashed over the rim of his cup and onto his lap.

Hands on hips and a frown on her face, she stood like a delicate Xena, warrior princess. "See anything you like?" She looked so incensed he couldn't help but laugh.

He was nothing if not honest, sometimes to his detriment. "Yes, I did." He grabbed the cloth from the floor and dabbed at the wet spot on his Wranglers. This would mean a return trip to his bedroom for dry jeans, but it was worth the inconvenience. He took a second to stare at her, drinking in the exotic look of dark eyes and white hair.

"I need to change clothes. How long until breakfast is done?" As he watched, she tried unsuccessfully to stop the smile blooming on her face. He was going to have to get this woman off his ranch before he made a total fool of himself. Aw, hell. Who was he kidding? He didn't want her to leave.

"The men will be here in half an hour. If you hurry, I'll take care of you first."

Her words caused the blood in his veins to heat. A mental picture of her kneeling before him, taking care of him, set his brain on fire. He turned and hurried upstairs before she saw the effect she had on him. "Dammit all to hell."

"You're not supposed to swear, Pa." Willa Wild stood in the hall outside her bedroom door. She had the hem of her turquoise Elsa nightie clutched in one hand to keep it from dragging on the floor. Her curly red hair was as wild as her name.

A tomboy during the day, his daughter was all princess at night. Micah knelt beside her and pulled her into his arms. "Thanks for reminding me. Come on. Let's get you dressed. Goodun needs someone to take him outside."

By the time Willa and Micah were both dressed the ranch hands had made it into breakfast. Willa Wild raced into the kitchen. He could hear her sweet voice as she greeted her friends. His daughter had never met a stranger.

"Hi, boss." Barnsey stood in one corner of the kitchen with a plate piled high with food. Two of the younger men were talking to Willa and the puppy. The rest of the men crowded around the table waiting for breakfast.

Cary pulled another casserole pan from the oven and replaced the empty one on the table. Before she could move away, the men refilled their plates. "Good stuff, Ms. Cary," one of the men replied.

Micah grabbed a plate from the stack. If he didn't get his butt in gear, the food would be gone. The aroma of sausage, eggs and salsa filled his nostrils. This was one of his gram's recipes. And it was every bit as good as when she'd made it.

As he spooned the food into his mouth, he looked up to find Cary watching him. She bit her lip and quickly turned away. Micah shoveled the last forkful into his mouth, and put the plate in the sink. "This hit the spot. Thanks for taking care of me." When she jerked her head up, he laughed. "And all the other men."

As her face grew red, she slapped at him with the dishtowel.

"Wait, no. I didn't mean that the way it sounded." At his raised voice, the others stopped talking and looked at them. "I meant cooking for the crew."

She nodded and began cleaning the table. One by one, after complimenting Cary, the other men left the kitchen. Cary refused to look at him and made a show of filling the dishwasher.

"Cary." He moved closer, until his shoulder touched hers. He bent close and whispered in her ear. "I'm sorry."

The strident sound of a familiar voice sent an electric shock down his spine and he jerked away.

"This is a cozy little picture. I see you've moved in my replacement."

Marlene stood just inside the back door. Her hair, so like Willa Wild's, bloomed in a curly red crown around her head. Dressed in stiletto boots and leggings, her sapphire silk top was cut low to show off her assets. She looked more striking than when she'd left. Being alone must agree with her.

No wait. She'd been single for years, but he'd bet his best hat she hadn't been alone for a minute.

Marlene walked across the room, her hips swaying in the way that used to scramble his brain. She sidled up to him and pressed a quick kiss to his cheek. "Hi, baby."

"What do you want?" He took a step back, putting distance between them. There'd been a time when he couldn't keep his hands off her. He'd thought in terms of forever, but for Marlene, the chase was more rewarding than the prize. "You're a week early for your visit with your daughter."

She closed the distance and ran her finger across his lips and down his chest. "Did it ever occur to you that I might be missing her? And you?" When she tried to step even closer, he grabbed her wrist and pulled her toward the living room. There was no need for Cary to witness their interaction.

When they reached the doorway, Marlene pulled free and turned back to Cary. "I think it'd be best if you stayed away from my husband!"

## 6

Cary heard raised voices coming from the living room, but the words didn't register. She picked up the washcloth, rung it out then scrubbed the counter as if the task would fix the unfixable.

Looking down at her hands, she stopped. In one swift movement, she turned and fired the wet rag across the room. It splatted against the window in the back door then slid to the floor.

He was married. The bastard had a wife, and he'd kissed her—twice.

And even worse. She'd kissed him back.

Cary retrieved the rag and put it in the laundry room. She grabbed a fresh one from the drawer and rinsed the large yellow bowl. She couldn't think about this now.

Baking had been the one constant in her life, the one thing that didn't change. It hadn't taken long enough to finish the apple cake, so she looked around for something harder.

Soufflé was one of her favorites. But even the thought of the creamy goodness couldn't pull her thoughts from Micah.

She couldn't hear him or his wife anymore. Maybe they'd left. Maybe they'd gone outside, or maybe as her over-active brain suggested, they'd gone upstairs.

She stopped what she was doing. It was time she left. She'd have earned enough money to get her a few hundred more miles. On the drive cross-country, she could earn gas money working at one back roads café or another.

Although it pained her to throw out the makings for the souffle, she dumped it into the garbage. After she'd washed the bowl, she tiptoed to the doorway into the living room. It was empty.

She'd have liked to throw what she owned into her duffle and leave before Micah came back, but she needed the money she'd earned. Unsure what to do, she sat on the bed, wondering about this place and the man who lived here.

Despite her city upbringing, this was the first place she'd felt she belonged. In the few days since she'd arrived, she'd become attached to Willa Wild West. The name didn't fit the girl. She was as sweet as any child Cary had ever met.

At the sound of gravel hitting the house, Cary stood and moved to the window. Micah's pickup roared out of the driveway. Fixing her eyes on the barn, she saw the calves playing in the pen. She'd miss the animals and the rolling hills. She'd miss Micah.

Enough! There would be no missing that man. *That married man*, she corrected.

She barely had enough money to buy a tank of gas and food for a few days, but she had to leave now. She could write and ask him to send the rest of her money after she was far from the ranch. Straightening her spine and strengthening her mind, she stuffed her few belongings in her bag and ran down the stairs.

It looked like for once luck would be with her. She didn't see anyone as she stowed her bags in the trunk of the green car. The red electrician's tape that masked the crushed tail-light had curled away from the metal. She pressed it back into place. It would have to do until she got to another town.

Cary smoothed out the towel that covered the ripped upholstery and slid behind the steering wheel. She took one more look at the house and barnyard before turning the key. Once again, she didn't belong, and it was time to go.

The drive into town took what seemed to be mere minutes. The only thing she needed to do was gas up the Focus before heading down the road. She pulled up to the pumps in front of the Co-op.

She'd watched Micah charge a tank of fuel the first day she was here. He owed her six days work. She was sure he wouldn't mind if she took a few gallons as part of her pay.

The teenager behind the cash register narrowed his eyes when she told him she wanted to charge a tank of gas. He opened a notebook then shook his head. "Sorry ma'am. You're not on our approved list.

What was with this town? Was everyone this suspicious of newcomers? Cary pulled out her wallet. With no choice but to spend the last of her money, she laid the bills on the counter. As she pushed them toward the kid, a large, rough hand stopped her.

Micah stood beside her, his face grim, his hand on her arm. He spoke without taking his eyes off hers. "Tom, would you fill up Ms. Crockett's car, please."

The boy's face flushed red.

"And from now on, Cary can charge anything she wants."

The young man nodded as he hurried out to the pumps, leaving them alone in the store.

"Leaving so soon?" Micah stood back, folding his arms across his chest. The arms of the T-shirt he wore stretched across his biceps, the muscles in his shoulders strained the fabric. "You could have at least said good-bye."

The look on his face tightened her lungs into a miserable knot. She struggled to pull in a breath. "Your wife is back. You don't need me." God, had she ever seen a more handsome man or sounded more pathetic?

"Marlene has nothing to do with you." He leaned against the counter. "She's not a cook."

And there it was. Three strikes of stupidity for her in the last hour. A new record.

She'd thought he liked her. She'd thought he'd come after her. She'd even thought about staying before Marlene showed up.

Micah wasn't asking her to come back because of any attraction. He wanted a cook, plain and simple, and if he had any other choice, he wouldn't be here now.

She closed her eyes and concentrated on the logical side of her brain. Being a cook was what she wanted, too. To be just a cook and make enough money to escape Mad Dog.

"If I come back, you'll have to explain to her that I'm no threat. I don't mess around with married men." Cary put the bills back into her wallet then looked him in the eye. "Ever."

"Let's clear something up. We're not married and haven't been for six years." He stepped behind her and placed his hand on the small of her back, steering her toward the door. "Let's go."

Cary hurried, moving away from his touch as she walked out to the car. The red tape laid in a wadded mess below the taillight. She tried to smooth it back into place but the edges refused to stick to the fender. Tossing it in the trashcan, she climbed into her car.

Micah leaned down, his arms resting on the driver's side door. "What year is this?" The pungent odor of hay and horses wafted in the window.

How could that make this man smell so good? She tore her gaze away from him and dug for the keys in her purse. "Two thousand."

"See you at the ranch." With a nod, he walked to his truck.

The drive into town felt like it took minutes, but the drive back seemed to take hours. When Cary arrived at the ranch, she leaned against the front of the car and enjoyed the warm air. For the first time in her life, she knew where she wanted to belong, but she had no idea how to achieve what that.

But sitting here wishing wasn't accomplishing anything. Time to go inside and prepare dinner.

As she mounted the steps, she caught sight of Marlene rocking at the far end of the porch. Cary pretended not to notice, but Marlene followed her into the kitchen.

"Micah tried to tell me you're nothing but the cook. He's a fool. I can see the way you look at him, and it isn't an employee to boss kind of way." She opened the refrigerator and pulled out a can of Diet Coke. "He likes to fool around, but he always comes back."

Anger warred with embarrassment as the emotions raced through her body. She wanted to tell this obnoxious woman she was wrong, but when Micah had kissed her, she hadn't protested.

"I'm the mother of his child." Marlene took a bottle of Jack Daniels from the pantry and poured a healthy dose into the pop can. She turned to face Cary. "That will never change." With a self-satisfied smile, she left Cary struggling for words.

"I don't want your husband or anyone's husband," Cary said to the empty room. "I'm doing fine on my own." Why did her mind always go blank when confronted with an attack? Why did she always think of something to say when the other person had left? Because she wasn't doing fine, and a big part of her wanted a man like Micah.

IT HAD ONLY TAKEN a few minutes to install the new bulb and taillight cover on Cary's car. He couldn't do anything about the crumpled metal on the side of the fender, but now she wouldn't get a ticket for having the light out. After wiping the plastic lens free of dust, he gathered his tools then headed for the barn. He'd converted the end stall into a workshop when he was still in high school. He hung the screwdriver on the pegboard wall, and turned to find Marlene standing in the doorway.

"What do you want?" Their relationship had been antagonistic since she'd left him and Willa Wild, but this visit was the worst yet. He tried to brush by, but she grabbed his belt and pulled him back.

"Don't you have a few minutes to talk?" Marlene ran her hand down his arm and smiled. "I need to ask a tiny little favor."

Micah leaned back against the wall and stuffed his hands in the front pockets of his jeans. He couldn't count the number of times he'd fantasized about never having met this woman. Wished that he'd walked away when she'd come up to him in the bar so many years ago. But if he had, he wouldn't have Willa, and he'd put up with any amount of irritation and scheming to have his daughter. "What now?"

He could read her like a book, and she wanted something she didn't think he'd give.

"Well, you see. I've been working on a film."

His bark of laughter wiped the smile from her face. "Working?"

"No, hear me out. It's about a group of Texas women trying to make it on their own, and how hard it is." She pouted, her eyes filling with tears. "They are late paying me."

"You've never been on your own." Only after they'd married had he found out she'd moved from boyfriends to sugar daddies with ease. He'd been the only one foolish to make her his wife.

"Micah!"

He pulled out his wallet. "How much do you need this time?"

She placed her hand over his, and lifted to give him a kiss on the cheek. "Oh, I can't take your money."

He jerked away. "Since when?" Pulling out a hundred dollar bill, he held it out to her.

The shocked look on her face made him laugh. Her eyes narrowed and she pursed her lips. "Put that away." Marlene walked to the bench in the aisle and sat down.

She looked desperate, but Micah had seen her acting skills on more than one occasion. The film should have been right up her alley. She should have been on Broadway. "Again, what do you want?"

"I need a place to stay for a while." She sat with her forearms on her knees. Raising her head, she hurried on trying to get the words out before he cut her off. "Not for too long, and I won't cause any problems. Please."

"No." The last thing Micah wanted was to be around this

woman twenty-four hours a day or even twenty-four minutes.

"Please, I have nowhere else to go." Marlene got on her knees in the dust, and held her hands up to him. She was begging. "Think of Willa Wild."

Anger burned through him like a wild fire on a windy day. He grabbed her arm and pulled her to her feet. "Think of Willa? When have you ever thought of your daughter?" Even as he raged at her, he knew he'd let her stay. He was caught like a coyote in a snare trap. The first thing she'd do was to tell Willa he'd kicked her mama out. Make him look like the bad guy. One day he'd have to explain to his daughter about her mother, but not today. "How long?"

"Only a week. I told them to send the check here and as soon as I get it, I'll be gone." A wide grin spread across her flawless face. She'd gotten her way and everything was right in her world. "You won't even know I'm here."

"One week."

She threw herself at him in an attempt to give him a hug, but he stepped back. "Stay out of my way." Turning, he hurried out of the barn. He'd never make it a whole week with Marlene living in the same house.

What in the hell had he done to deserve that devious woman? Sure, he could be a jackass sometimes, but he tried to be honest and fair. She was the gag gift that kept on giving. He stormed up the back steps. Frustration caused him to overreact, and he threw the door open, slamming against the wall.

Cary dropped a large bowl and chopped vegetables scattered across the floor. Goodun woke from his nap by the pantry and rushed toward Micah, the hair on the nape of his neck ruffled. He bounced around Micah's feet. Those high-pitched growls would be scary one day, but right now, they were all bluff.

It was the fear on Cary's face that caught him by surprise. She started toward the living room at a run. He heard her cry out as she tripped over the scatter rug.

Micah hurried to help her get up, stepping over an angry Goodun, but she scooted to the fireplace and grabbed a piece of kindling. "Get away!" She scrambled to her knees, holding the wood like a baseball bat.

He stopped and squatted in front of her. "Take it easy. I'm not going to hurt you." He held out one hand, but she swatted it away.

"Damn right, you're not." Fear and determination rolled off her in waves. She struggled to her feet, never taking her eyes off him.

Someone had done a job on her. Micah rose slowly then took a couple of steps back, giving her some room. "Cary, I'm not going to hurt you." He sat on the couch, hoping he presented a less threatening figure.

She dropped her arm to her side, and reached down to pick up the puppy. Her eyes remained wary, but he didn't think she'd hit him now. "You scared me," she said, her voice a whisper, her hand stroking the soft fur. "Don't do that again."

He couldn't contain his laughter. As soon as the sound came out, he realized he should have tried harder. "I won't. Are you all right?"

"This isn't funny." Her hands were shaking, and she looked like she might collapse onto the floor.

"It's not." He nodded to the rocker. "Sit down, please."

Her gaze darted to the chair then back to him. She must have decided he wouldn't attack her, and she lowered herself into the chair still holding the piece of wood.

"Want to put the kindling back in the box?"

She nodded then froze. "I . . . I'm . . ." The wood hit the floor with a loud clatter and rolled beneath the oak side table. Cary's eyes were wide, and she put the pup on the floor.

In two steps he was by her side. Her face had faded to a nasty shade of gray. He pushed her head between her knees then gently kneaded her shoulders. "You'll be okay in a minute. Just relax."

When she raised her head, some of the color was back in her cheeks.

"Better?" Micah looked up as the front door creaked.

Marlene stood just inside the door, a small smile on her face. "Am I interrupting?"

## 7

Wasn't that just a homey scene? The western décor set off the picture of Micah almost in a clinch with his so-called cook. The sight of her husband—make that ex-husband but he was hers none the less—kneeling over that Cary woman, his arm around her shoulders, made Marlene's chest tighten and her blood pressure rise.

She'd heard rumors of Micah dating one local girl or another after she'd left for Dallas, but he'd never been serious and the relationships hadn't lasted over a few months. There'd always been a room for her when she came home. And this was her home.

The look he gave Cary set off warning bells in her brain. No way was she letting this blonde move in on her territory. Marlene couldn't stay with Micah and their daughter full time. She'd wither and grow old here on the ranch, but she didn't want to give up her place here either. These people were her safety net.

"Marlene, you'd better think about what you're going to

say." Micah held her gaze a moment then turned back to Cary.

Cary drew in a deep breath and closed her eyes. Bracing her hands on the chair, she stood, hanging on until her legs stopped shaking. "I'm fine. I'll just go upstairs for a few minutes."

Micah's hands lightly touched her waist, ready to catch her if she fell. "You'll sit here and make sure you're okay." He placed his hands on her shoulders and gently pushed her onto the couch.

Marlene's first instinct was to shift into attack mode, but she remembered the talk they'd had in the barn. Micah had warned her. It took a lot to piss Micah off, but when he made up his mind, there was no changing it.

She pasted a sympathetic expression on her face and hurried across the room, giving them her best, worried look. "Are you all right, honey? Can I get you anything?"

Apprehension still lingered in Cary's eyes and as Marlene thrust out her hand, Cary ducked her head before she caught herself. Marlene saw real fear, not a made-up emotion to get Micah's sympathy. This might make for an interesting couple of weeks. Someone had done a number on the cook.

"I'm fine—really." Cary ran her fingers through that white blonde hair, causing it to stick out in all directions.

Even messed up, she looked exotic. It wasn't fair. Marlene was pretty in a hometown girl kind of way, but she'd always wanted to be so much more. Maybe she'd try biker boots.

"Let me get you a glass of water." Micah hurried away.

Marlene sat on the floor beside Cary. "Did you fall?" She was dying to know how Cary ended up on the floor with Micah playing caretaker. "Or trip?"

"No—well, yes. Kind of." Cary leaned her head against the brown leather of the sofa and pulled Goodun into her lap. Her eyes closed, and she gave a soft sigh.

What was she hiding? She couldn't have given a more ambiguous answer if she'd tried. Marlene loved a mystery. As she studied Cary, the front door sailed open and slammed against the wall.

Cary nearly fell off the couch. Her hand flew to her mouth.

"We gots new babies. Lots of 'em." Willa Wild rushed into the room. The curly red hair Marlene had braided just after she'd arrived had come undone and floated around the freckled face like Medusa's locks.

"Willa Wild, you go back out the door and come in like a lady." Marlene stood and gave the child her best mom-look. She was of out of practice, but her daughter got the message.

"Mama, I'm a cowgirl, not a lady. Ask Pa." She stomped one little cowboy boot.

The move might have been more effective if she hadn't had a pink tutu over her jeans. When Marlene put her hands on her hips, her daughter shrugged then walked outside, the toes of her boots dragging along the red tile of the entryway. A second after the door closed, it opened again without the bang. With exaggerated sweetness, she bowed to Marlene and Cary. "Hi, ladies." The frown from a moment ago was gone, and the smile was back.

Marlene smiled in return. She didn't know how it had happened, but her daughter was the happiest child ever born. "Tell Ms. Crockett you're sorry you scared her."

"I scared you?" Willa Wild ran over to Cary and plopped down beside her. She scooted her butt into the space between Cary and the arm of the couch and scratched the puppy behind the ears. "I'm sorry. I was excited."

"It's okay. What were you saying about the babies? Puppies, kittens or calves?"

Marlene stood back and watched the interaction between her daughter and the woman. Cary seemed genuinely interested in what Willa Wild said. She had to give the cook points for making the girl believe she was listening.

"Calves, three of them. One is black, and one is red, but the best one has speckles all over its butt." Willa turned to her mother. "I'm calling it Frosty. Barnsey let me pet Frosty."

She'd tried to make her daughter a lady, but it was as if the girl had been born one of the ranch creatures. Being here only once every few months made it harder, but Marlene was determined. "Go wash your hands then come back, and we'll help Cary with dinner."

When the little girl had left the room, Marlene got right to the point. "We might be separated, but he's still mine." She waited to see what Cary would say. One thing Marlene was good at was reading people.

Cary drew in a sharp breath, a bright flush covering her cheeks.

Gotcha!

Cary stood and turned on Marlene, one hand balled into a fist, the other grasping the puppy to her side. "How about you take care of your life, and I'll take care of mine, and mine doesn't include Micah." She turned and hurried toward the kitchen, side-stepping Micah as he came back with a glass of water.

Micah watched Cary then turned to Marlene. "What did you say now?"

"Nothing. Cary seems upset about something. I'm

worried about her." When Micah shook his head and left, she headed for the stairs. It was time to go into full diva mode and get rid of this interloper.

Riffling through her closet, Marlene chose then discarded one outfit after another. When she touched the red floral summer dress, she knew. She'd worn this dress the day Micah had proposed. She'd often wondered why she kept the thing. Guess her sub-conscious knew she'd have a use for it one day.

With her hair flowing loose and the dress hugging her body, Marlene went to find her husband. Just as she'd expected, he was in the kitchen helping Cary clean up the mess she'd made when she dropped the bowl of vegetables.

Marlene stood in the door and waited. "Can I help?" She turned on her southern accent. The one Micah had loved when they'd first met. When Marlene wanted to be nice, she could be sweeter than a cherry pie at a summer picnic.

When Micah looked up, his gaze locked on her body and a delicious shiver went up her spine. She still had it.

"What can I do?" She moved into the room, her hips swaying. She lifted her hair and pushed it back over her shoulders. "Cary, you should be laying down. I'll cook."

A sharp bark of laughter came from Micah.

One of Marlene's natural born talents was pushing things too far. Offering to cook might send Micah over the edge. "I can make sandwiches, Micah."

"If someone shows you where the bread is." Micah stood and dumped the veggies in the trash then turned to her, the look of appreciation gone. "During our marriage, you'd have starved rather than cook. What are you up to?"

≈

CARY POURED four blobs of pancake batter onto the large griddle then turned to flip the bacon. Caffeine from two cups of black coffee coursed through her veins. The magic elixir was a necessity this morning. She should have gone back downstairs last night, but after hearing the angry voices, she didn't have the energy to listen to Micah and Marlene bicker for another minute. When the adrenaline from her scare dissipated, she'd been overcome with exhaustion. Still, she spent a big portion of the night wondering about the people on this ranch.

Cary heard scratching at the door and opened it to let Goodun in. Maybe it was because she loved the pup or the fact that he was her first pet, but she thought he must be smarter than other puppies his age.

Goodun wagged his stubby tail then walked to the old towels Micah had used to make him a bed. Turning three times, he plopped down and closed his eyes. She didn't know how she'd keep him, but she wasn't giving him up no matter which path she chose for herself.

Walking back to the breakfast fixings, Cary wondered how Marlene fit in to this household. She was Willa Wild's mother, sure, but how did Micah feel about his ex-wife? He'd told Cary there was nothing between them, and he didn't seem to have a civil word to say to Marlene. The fact remained, the woman had her own room, and according to Willa Wild, her mama seemed to come back to stay whenever she felt like it.

And then there was Micah. Attractive in a rough, cowboy way, he brought up visions of a home and babies. In another time and place, she might have time to get to know him, but Marlene had made it clear they still had something going.

Another sip of coffee didn't do much for the jitters she'd woken with this morning. Lack of sleep did that to her. The thought of seeing Micah added to her anxious feeling. His touch sent tingles across her nerve endings; his scent warmed her to the core.

She stacked pancakes on a platter and turned to the bacon. As she transferred food to the table, one piece of bacon dropped. Goodun was on it before it touched the linoleum.

"Quick little bugger." At the sound of Micah's deep voice, she almost dropped the pancakes.

She looked at the cowboy then back to the puppy. Goodun crouched over the meat, growling with a high-pitched puppy sound. "He will be a good watch dog."

"If you ask him to guard bacon." Micah sat at the table and forked a pile of pancakes and half a pound of pork onto his plate. "I'm going into town this morning. Want to come along?"

In the week she'd spent here, she'd gotten a better handle on the kinds and amounts of food needed to keep the ranch running. "Sure. I've been keeping a list of things I need."

"As soon as the men are done meet me out back." Micah stacked his dishes in the sink and disappeared toward his office.

It still amazed Cary how fast these men could put away mounds of food, but within a half hour the kitchen was empty, and she worked to clean it. She'd just wiped off the table when Micah appeared.

"I've got to finish tonight's dinner. Give me a minute." Cary sat two crockpots on the counter. After filling each one with a roast, potatoes and carrots, she sprinkled the spice packets on top then added beef broth. No way would the men go hungry tonight. She washed her hands then followed Micah to the truck.

They didn't say much on the drive into town. Caught up in her own thoughts, it was kind of nice settling into a comfortable silence.

Micah pulled to the curb in front of the grocery and turned off the key. "Got your list?"

Cary nodded. This was the third time she'd been to East Hope. The first time, she'd only seen the restaurant and spent a short time in the store. The second, she'd tried to use Micah's credit at the co-op. This time, she wanted to look around the town and get to know some of the people.

She climbed out of Micah's pickup and looked around the small town. East Hope's buildings were old and time-worn, but its streets were clean, and it was obvious the townspeople cared about their city.

As if he read her mind, Micah took her hand and led her toward the bank. The two-story, red brick building had new white shutters and a large welcome mat. A balding man dressed in a suit came forward to greet them.

"Hank, I'd like to introduce Cary Crockett. Cary, this is Hank Loveland. Hank runs the bank."

Cary stuck out her hand like she'd seen the locals do and smiled. "Nice to meet you, Mr. Loveland."

"Well, this is just a pleasure, Ms. Crockett." He was friendly, but Cary got the feeling he didn't trust easily. Must be something in the water. Distrust seemed to be ingrained in these people. "And I have to correct Micah here. I don't just run the bank, I'm the president."

"Cary is cooking for the boys. You got the papers ready?" Micah's mood shifted from open to suspicious.

"I'll have them Thursday, Micah. I'm sorry for the delay." Hank's attitude became even more effusive. "Ms. Crockett, how long are you here for?"

Cary glanced at Micah. His frown was as dark as a thunderstorm. "Remember what I said Hank." He turned without another word and walked out, with Cary chasing after him.

"What's wrong?" His long strides outdistanced her so she jogged a few steps to catch up. When he didn't slow down, she placed her hand on his forearm. "Micah?"

"Sorry. That pompous ass gets to me. We were friends in high school, but now that he's head of the bank, he thinks he knows everything." He stopped then looked around town. "I'm hungry."

"You're always hungry."

Without a word, he took her hand and led her toward the Five and Diner. "I'll introduce you to Cal. He's the cook I tried to hire that day you first showed up in East Hope."

Micah didn't release her hand. Most of the time when Ken had touched her, he'd wanted something from her. It was never to savor her skin against his. For the few moments it took them to reach the café, she could pretend Micah's touch meant something.

They reached the door. Micah held it open then led her to a table by the window. Dust covered landscapes made from bits of bark and pine needles hung on the walls, all signed by the artist. Originally red, the tabletops had faded to a nondescript pink, and the red vinyl on several of the stools at the counter was mended with the same tape she'd used for her taillight. Nothing much had changed since she'd been here a few days ago. Nothing much had changed in the last fifty years from the look of the place.

Cary looked up from the menu to see a woman who most likely kept Avon in business.

Her up-do was the flat black of a home-dye job. Too many layers to count of black mascara covered her lashes.

Sparkly, azure blue eye shadow and navy eyeliner framed her eyes and frosty pink lipstick tinted her lips.

She slammed two glasses of water on the table then stood back, her arms crossed beneath her ample chest. *No Farms, No Food* stretched across the front of her Kelly green t-shirt. "Micah West, you're about as welcome here as a skunk at a lawn party."

"Hi, Lorna. I'm glad to see you, too." Micah didn't even look up. He pointed at a line on the menu. "I'll have the chicken fried steak with fries and a piece of your delicious cherry pie."

"I've a mind not to serve you at all. The way you tried to take Cal away from me, I'd as soon bite a bug as serve you." She turned on Cary. "You with him?"

"If it means I won't get served, I'm not."

"This guy ever gives you trouble, you call on me." The woman winked at Cary then turned back to Micah. "Well—"

Micah's face softened into a smile. "Can't we call it a momentary lapse in judgment brought on by severe stress?"

"I suppose I can forgive you this time." She pulled her order pad from the pocket of her ruffled plaid apron then pointed at him with her pen. "This time."

When Lorna's attention returned to Cary, she ordered. "I'll have the same, but with lemon meringue, please."

Cary assumed Lorna had forgiven Micah because the food arrived in minutes and was some of the best she'd ever eaten. They talked about unimportant things until Micah asked about her family. She hated talking about this stuff, so she gave him the shortened version of her life. "I don't know where my dad is. I don't remember ever meeting him." The look on his face said pity in capital letters, and she couldn't have that. "I also don't miss him. My mom and I got along just fine."

Micah nodded as he worked his fork into the pie. "Sounds like you and she are close."

"Some people would say that." She took a big bite. "Why don't you tell me about your wife?" A dusky flush worked its way over his cheeks. Good, she wasn't the only one uncomfortable with the questions.

"I told you. Marlene's not my wife. She hasn't been since Willa Wild was small." His attention appeared focused on getting every last bit of the cherry pie off his plate.

Cary laid down her fork. She folded her hands in her lap. "Are you sure she knows that?"

Micah's fork clattered as he dropped it to the plate then pushed it to the center of the table. "She left us. Enough said."

He might think that's all that needed to be said, but his words made Cary wonder why he let her continue to come back. But she knew. Marlene was Willa Wild's mother, and she knew better than most that a girl needed a mom. Even though Micah and Marlene were divorced, there didn't appear to be room for Cary in this scenario.

"Any brothers or sisters?"

She stuffed a huge piece of her pie into her mouth. Maybe if he saw her chewing he'd stop the questioning, but he waited while she swallowed. "No. Just me and mom."

"Where's your mother now?" He wadded up his napkin and waited for her answer.

She should lie. She could make up any answer, and he'd never know the difference. But the words wouldn't come out of her mouth. She couldn't lie to Micah. "I don't know."

## 8

The muscles in her jaw had clenched as her knuckles turned white when she grasped her fork. He'd hit a nerve. "Let's go check out the rest of the town. If you're going to be here a while, you might as well meet some townspeople." Micah threw a few bills on the table then stood and held out his hand.

Cary stared at his outstretched fingers then looked away, keeping her hands to herself. The satisfaction he'd felt holding her hand as they crossed the street was real, and he wasn't giving up on her now. They walked along the sidewalk on the main street of town until they came to the feed store. "Want to look around?"

When she smiled at him, his heart kicked up a notch.

"Sure. Who wouldn't want to shop at the feed and seed?" She pulled open the glass door and went inside. Cary wandered the aisles while Micah paid his bill.

A young man came out from behind the counter.

"Tom, you remember Ms. Crockett from the other day?" Micah came up behind her and placed his hand on her shoulder. "Cary, this is Tom Hart."

"I remember you. Nice to see you again, Tom," Cary said, a bright smile on her face. "I'm looking for cake pans. I don't suppose you have any of those here."

Micah watched as Tom fell under Cary's spell. He knew just how the kid felt. While they took off for the cooking section of the store that had most everything a person could want, Micah ordered the supplies he needed for the ranch.

With Cary clutching a bag with the pans, they walked back to the truck. Micah pointed outed bits of information about East Hope.

Cary nodded or gave him one-word answers.

"Cary." He stopped and waited until she made eye contact. "You can tell me about your mother if and when you feel comfortable talking about her."

She blinked rapidly and turned away. "Tell me how East Hope got its name."

Obviously she wasn't ready yet. He looked down the short main street. East Hope looked like any other small town across the country, but this was his town. He couldn't imagine living anywhere else. "Originally this was the town of Hope. Founded and named by a couple of brothers around 1850 in hopes of finding gold. That never happened, and when they had a falling out, one moved to one end of town and one to the other. You can guess the rest."

Cary had watched him as he spoke, her brow furrowed. "If this is East Hope, where's West Hope?"

"It just kind of faded away. Only us East Hopeians left." He pointed to the west. "About three miles down the highway are the abandoned feed store and livery."

"Interesting." She looked up. "What's next?"

"Groceries." They settled the supplies they'd bought at the Co-op into the back of the truck then entered Foodtown.

Cary dug into her pocket and pulled out a list.

"What you got there?"

Everything was grouped by type and listed alphabetically. Under fruit, she had apples, bananas, and blueberries. For vegetables — broccoli, corn, lettuce, potatoes and tomatoes. Staples were the longest list, including baking powder, cheese, flour, pasta, sugar (brown and white), and vinegar.

"These are all in order. Are you this organized with everything?" He looked up with a smile to see her cheeks brightening to a soft pink.

She snatched back the list and turned away from his frank appraisal.

Micah took hold of her arm and turned her to face him. "Hey, I didn't mean to embarrass you. I was just asking." Cary was tough most of the time, but she had some triggers.

"It's no big deal. I admit I like things in order." She pulled a breath in and let it out on a sigh. "I'm going to grab a cart."

As Cary disappeared around the corner, Millie came around the end of the aisle. She hurried toward him and gave him a big hug. "Bout time you came in again. Just got a big supply of chocolate-covered raisins. Your favorite." She took his hand and pulled.

"Wait, a minute." The wobbly wheels of the grocery cart clattered against the chipped linoleum floor as Cary came up behind them. "Millie, you remember Cary?"

The older woman froze, her expression changing from friendly to frigid. "You're still here." It wasn't a question, and it wasn't welcoming and it wasn't like Millie at all.

Micah had never seen Millie react to a person as she did to Cary. Suspicion wafted off her in waves, annoyance darkened her friendly appearance.

Millie switched her focus back to Micah. "The candy is back here."

Micah looked at Cary. There wasn't much he could say. If Millie didn't like Cary, he couldn't change her mind. He would ask Millie what was going on—another day. "Sorry about that. I don't know what's with her."

"Or what was with her the last time I was here." Cary shrugged. "I rarely have this effect on people."

He grinned. "Now let's see. So far you've made an enemy of Marlene, Millie and a couple of the hands."

He could see she was trying to keep the insulted look on her face but humor broke through. "I don't think Marlene counts."

"You've got a point there. Marlene is—Marlene." He plucked the list from her hand and tore it in half. "You take care of this. I'll get the rest."

Micah found Millie in the storage area in the back of the store. She'd ripped open a cardboard box and opened the plastic bag. There must be twenty pounds of chocolate-covered raisins inside. With a large scoop, Millie filled a white paper bag then handed it to him.

"That's a lot of goodness right there." He reached in and grabbed a handful, his mouth watering, anticipating the taste.

Millie's pale blue eyes squinted as her rosy cheeks lifted with her smile. She gave him a soft punch in the shoulder. "They're not all for you. Some other people in town like them, too."

"Given enough time, I bet I could eat all of them." He tossed a couple more of the candies into his mouth. "What's in the other boxes?"

Millie took her box cutter and opened another box. This one was filled with chocolate covered orange sticks. "I got four different kinds. The other two have nuts." She held out the square candy. "This is my favorite."

Micah had her give him a bag of the orange candy, too. "I wonder what kind Cary would like?"

At the mention of Cary's name, Millie's smile faded from her face. She closed the candy boxes. "She'll just have to wait until I get these on display." The store owner turned and hurried out the back of the building. Micah followed her to the door. The outburst was about as out of character for his friend as he'd ever seen.

"Micah?" He heard Cary calling for him. He'd have to think about this. Did Millie see something off about Cary, something he didn't?

Cary stood by the meat cooler, her cart nearly full. "Have you got your groceries?"

"Haven't even started. Millie gave me some candy." He held out both bags. "Want some?"

"Millie's sweet on you, isn't she?"

This time it was Micah who was embarrassed. He'd considered once that Millie might have a crush on him, but it was easier to ignore a situation that could become awkward. He had no feelings for Millie other than those of a friend, but he didn't want to lose that. "We're friends."

"If you say so." Cary took one of the bags. "What are these?" She took a bite of the candy. "Oh my god, these are sugar overload."

"They are one of the truly wonderful concoctions known to man."

"They are sugar and preservatives."

"I can't believe a pastry chef doesn't like sugar." Micah popped a few more into his mouth.

"I don't hate sugar, but I make things from fresh ingredients not chemicals."

A can dropped to the floor, and they both turned to see Millie standing behind them, her face drawn into a frown.

"If you don't like what I sell here, feel free to shop some-where else." Millie stood with her arms crossed, her expression thunderous. With a great amount of effort, she looked at Micah. "Enjoy your raisins."

The venom in the woman's tone made Cary's heart race. What had she done to receive so much anger from a person she hardly knew? "What just happened here?"

"You shouldn't have insulted her candy."

Her head jerked up, and indignation threatened to drown her. "How is this my fault?" She grabbed the handle and shoved the cart toward the front of the store.

Micah followed. When they got to the checkout, Cary unloaded the groceries, placing canned goods onto the counter with a little more force than was necessary. Okay, more than a little.

The girl behind the register took a step back, her eyes wide.

Cary put the last can of beans on the counter. She looked at the cashier. "Would you ring this up? Micah will take care of it," she said then walked toward the door without a word.

She paced up and down in front of the pickup. When Micah stepped into her path, she twisted around him and continued.

"Can you calm down?" His voice was quiet as he leaned against the fender of the truck.

"No, I can't." She stopped, raising her gaze to stare into his eyes. "That woman insulted me, and you act like it's my fault. I had enough of being blamed for things with Ken. That's why he's no longer in my life."

"Ken?"

"My very ex-boyfriend." Cary turned her back to him. Let him think she was interested in what was happening down the street.

"Your ex-boyfriend? I thought you were married," Micah said, standing beside her, also scrutinizing the empty road. He sidestepped until his shoulder touched hers, causing a pleasant shiver to crawl down her arm.

"I'm not. And that doesn't excuse you for blaming me for Millie's bad behavior." She looked up at him and wasn't that a mistake. The sight of his blue eyes made her fingers curl.

"I didn't mean to blame you." The soothing sound of his voice almost made her give in. "I just meant that she takes her store very seriously, and you said you didn't like the candy."

"So, I don't have the right to an opinion, especially when it might hurt Millie's feelings. But it's okay for her to be rude to me? Is that what you're saying? Because if it is, you need to take me back to the ranch, and I'll be gone before sundown." Anger made it hard to breathe, and her chest heaved. She'd thought for a while that he was different, that he saw her, but he was like the rest, trying to stuff her into a hole where she didn't fit.

She'd opened her mouth to continue when Micah stepped forward. He put his hands on her cheeks and ran his thumb across her lips. "Shh," he said, just before he kissed her.

Her knees grew weak, and her hands lifted of their own accord to run through his hair. No matter how hard she tried to remain strong, his kisses melted her bones, and sent her brain on flights of fancy. She gave up and closed her eyes letting the feel and taste of Micah brighten her world.

A loud crash thundered through the air. Cary tried to jump away, but Micah's grip held her close.

Millie stood in the doorway to the store. The broken box spilled canned goods at her feet.

A can of beans rolled across the sidewalk and dropped off the curb into the street. The look Millie gave Cary chilled her.

"Your groceries." Millie disappeared into the store without another word, but Cary could just make out the woman watching from behind the window.

"If you'll get these, I'll get the food from the store."

Clinton Barnes' came up beside her as Micah hurried into the store. "Don't let Millie get to you," he said in his raspy voice. "She'll come around."

Cary watched as he entered the store and stopped to talk to Millie. It seemed like everyone worried about Millie. *Good old Millie. Everybody's friend.*

She carried the last of the cans to the truck and stacked them on the floorboard. If she wanted to stay here, and she needed to stay here for a few more weeks at the least, she'd find a way to be Millie's friend, too.

Micah arrived with the food from inside and added it to the truck. He nodded to the cab, and they both climbed inside. They drove for a few miles before Micah broke the silence. "Maybe you were right."

A giggle burst from Cary. "Maybe? Gee, thanks." The giggle turned to an outright laugh. She wanted to say more, but she was having a hard time catching her breath.

Pulling the truck off to the side of the road, Micha switched off the key and turned to her. He was trying hard to keep the smile from his face. "What's so funny?"

"You admitted you were wrong. Must be a hard thing to do, to climb down from your throne." She swiped at the wetness around her eyes and took several deep breaths, trying to regain control. She straightened her spine, but when she raised her gaze to him, a new round of laughter hit.

Micah started the truck and took off down a back road.

"Where are you going?" Cary barely got the words out between gasps.

"I'm taking you to the hospital. If you don't quit soon, you're going to need medical intervention for laughter overdose."

"Wait. Aren't we supposed to meet your foreman at home?"

"Clinton Barnes has been taking care of himself for longer than you've been alive."

"Looks to me like he could use some help with Millie." Cary reached into a bag of fruit and pulled out an orange. She worked the peel loose and stacked the bits in a neat pile in her lap, largest on the bottom, smallest on the top.

"Now you're alphabetizing the orange peel?" Micah glanced at the orange pyramid in her lap. "And what do you mean about Clint and Millie?"

No matter how hard Cary tried to control her slight OCD tendencies whenever she was tense they popped to the surface. Without looking at Micah, she put the peels into the grocery bag out of sight. "Didn't you see how Mr. Barnes watched Millie the first time we were in the store? He's got it bad."

Micah rolled up his window as they turned into the ranch driveway. Dust clouds rolled from beneath the tires and billowed out to cover everything within fifty yards with a blanket of gray. "I think you've been reading too many romance novels. Clint and Millie are friends, just friends."

She watched him. He believed what he said. The man

was oblivious to what was right in front of his face. Well, she wouldn't argue with him over something that didn't concern her. "If you say so."

"I've lived around these people my whole life. You've only been here a little over a week. I think I'd know if my friends were . . ." Micah stopped the truck beside the house. "What? Don't you have anything to say to that?"

Cary bit her lower lip. She should agree. She should stay out of the drama of small town life. She should, but she couldn't. "Have you ever bothered to ask Clint what he thinks of Millie? He's interested in her as more than a friend, and she'd like nothing better than to get it on with you. Open your eyes."

"Bullshit!"

## 9

Micah grabbed two boxes of groceries and made for the house. His first impression was proving to be correct for more than one reason. It was a terrible idea to hire Cary Crockett. Not only did she have the ranch hands mad about the meals every other day, now she was planting ideas in his head. No way was he going to get involved in Clint's life. The whole idea of Clint and Millie was ludicrous.

"Well, have you?" Cary followed him into the kitchen carrying a box filled with canned goods.

He'd thought they'd dropped the subject, but no such luck. "No, and I won't. It's none of my business."

"Is it your business to string Millie along and keep her from even looking at your friend?" Cary turned her back and put the canned goods onto the shelves in the pantry.

"I've got work to do." He stopped at the backdoor. "Do you need any help?"

"I've got it." She looked over her shoulder. "I'm sorry for butting in where I don't belong. It's a habit I'm trying to break."

He managed a slight smile before walking away. There were calves to feed and stalls to clean, and the work might get his mind off Cary for a few minutes.

As Micah crossed the barnyard, Clinton Barnes pulled the old red Ford pickup onto a patch of shade behind the barn and climbed out. Puffs of dust floated up from beneath his boots as he walked to the rear of the truck.

Should he ask the man about Millie? The thought of talking about touchy-feely things with an employee made shivers crawl down his spine. But Clinton Barnes was more than an employee. He was a friend.

"Get everything we need to fix the fences?"

"We're one bundle short of fence stays, but other than that we're good." Clint dropped the tailgate and pulled out one heavy roll of barbed wire and stacked it on the ground by the side of the barn.

Micah grabbed another roll and repeated the process.

Clint continued to work without saying a word, which wasn't unusual. Some days, Micah and Clint could work side by side for eight hours and not say more than a handful of words.

This time instead of it being a calm silence Micah got more nervous by the minute. Should he ask Clint how he felt about Millie? Shit! Even the word *feelings* gave him the heeby-jeebys. Maybe he'd wait for a while and see if things worked out between the two.

"You ever ask Millie out?" Where the hell had those words come from?

Clint's head jerked up, and he stared at Micah.

Now he'd gone and embarrassed himself worse than that day in junior high when he'd tried to impress Katy Sue. "Never mind. You don't have to answer that." Micah hurried to the other side of the truck bed and gathered an armful of fence stays.

He dropped the load beside the barbed wire and turned back to the pickup only to see Clint leaning against the truck fender, his arms crossed and his expression closed. "What made you ask that?"

"I'm sorry I did. Can we drop it?" Micah asked. As he watched, Clint's head shook slowly back and forth. "I have some things I have to do in the—" He couldn't go to the house, because Cary would want to discuss this very thing, and he couldn't go to the barn, because Clint was there.

"Why did you ask if I'd invited Millie out?" Clint hadn't moved, and Micah knew he wasn't going to let the subject go.

Micah sat on the tailgate. He pulled off his East Hope Feed & Seed cap, wiped his forehead with his forearm then settled the cap back on his head. "You're going to think this is funny. On the way home, Cary said she thought you liked Millie." God, he sounded like a junior high kid.

"Go on."

"That's it."

Clint unfolded his arms and grabbed two sacks of staples. Tossing them next to the barn, he added the T-post clips. After staring at Micah for a moment, he grabbed an armful of metal fence posts from the truck.

He waited for Clint to say more, but the man must have talked himself out. This had been a mistake. He'd known that from the moment the words left his mouth. "We'll start on this in the morning."

Clint nodded then went back to the posts.

Micah tried not to hurry away, tried not to look like he was fleeing the scene of a crime. As he opened the front door, Willa Wild met him.

"Pa, we're going on a picnic." She danced around him like a hyper active puppy.

The thought barely materialized when Goodun raced from the kitchen and skidded to a stop at his feet. Willa Wild yelled yippee, and the puppy let out a yip.

"Mama said we can go on a picnic to the lake, you and me and her. Oh, and Goodun. It's gonna be so much fun." She bounded up the stairs, but halfway she stopped and turned back. "We never get to do things together."

As his daughter disappeared up the stairs, Marlene came down, descending like a queen holding court. Her long red hair was loose and hung past her shoulders. Dressed in a red and white bikini, she twirled before wrapping a bright blue cloth around her hips. Leave it to Marlene to go on a picnic in a bikini even though it was much too cold to get in the water. She was pretty, but all he could see was a problem.

"Why did you tell Willa Wild we'd go on a picnic?" He watched as she crossed the room and sank onto the couch. "I don't have time for this."

Marlene made a show of flipping her hair over her shoulder. At one time he'd loved her long hair. "You don't have time for your daughter? I thought you were super-dad."

Life was a funny thing. There'd been a time that he couldn't get close enough to this woman. Now he wished there was a legal way to get her out of their lives.

"I'm not here much. I think the least you can do is let our daughter have a good time with her mother and father once a year." She gave him the cat smile she reserved for when she knew she had the upper hand. "Or, I can stay here more often."

And there it was. Her ace in the hole. If he played by her

rules, she only came around every few months. She probably wouldn't come around any more often if he didn't give
her what she wanted, but he didn't want to take a chance.
"How long is this going to take?"

She stood, and gave him the look that said she'd won. "A
couple of hours. You can spare that for your daughter, can't
you?" With a flip of her hand, she disappeared into the
kitchen.

Frustration flowed through every vein as he considered
spending two solid hours in Marlene's company. He could
do this if he concentrated on Willa.

"Pa," Willa called as she stomped down the stairs in her
bathing suit and her cowboy boots. "We can go swimming,
can't we? Mom's got her suit on, too."

The sight of her twig thin legs disappearing into the
scalloped top of her cowboy boots made him smile. She
stopped and struck a model pose. The turquoise suit hugged
her tiny body while the pink and white ruffle bobbed
around her hips. "Go get yours, Pa."

Micah picked up Willa Wild and smiled. "You know it's
too cold to go swimming in the lake." Her bottom lip stuck
out, and he took hold of it between his thumb and forefin-
ger. "You go get your jeans on, and I'll ask Cary if we can
take Goodun."

She wiggled in excitement, and when he put her down,
she clomped up the stairs as fast as she could go. Micah
walked into his office and closed the door. Today had been
one uncomfortable calamity after another. First Cary and
Millie, then his conversation with Clint and now, to top
things off, he had to pretend he was enjoying a day with
Marlene.

Why couldn't he spend the day with Cary and Willa

Wild? He sat in the big leather desk chair and let his imagi-
nation run wild.

As Cary marinated the steaks for dinner the next night, she
hummed Little Big Town's Pontoon and danced her way
around the kitchen to the music of her favorite song. Having
a carefree life with lots of friends like the characters in the
song was something she'd longed for and never had. Well,
she could pretend.

After checking the two large crockpots on the counter,
she grinned. The roasts for this evening's meal were coming
along nicely. Fresh green beans with bacon simmered on the
stovetop. She peeked through the glass in the oven door to
see if the cheesecake was done.

There would be no complaints from the hands about
tonight's meal.

"I need you to make a picnic lunch for today." Marlene
stood just inside the door, her hands on her hips. "I need it
to be special, and I need it in a half hour."

Cary rose slowly and turned to face Willa's mother. She
hadn't decided what Marlene was to Micah. "Kind of short
notice."

Marlene walked to the refrigerator and pulled out a Diet
Coke. Dressed in a red and white polka dot bikini top and a
deep blue sarong, she looked like she'd stepped out of a
Victoria's Secret swimsuit ad. "Micah told me you could fix
us something to take to the lake. You are the cook, right?"

The woman had her there, and if Micah wanted a picnic,
she'd provide one. The task would be easier if a sharp pain
didn't shoot through her heart at the thought of Micah and
Marlene. He'd told her there was nothing between them,

but it looked like he'd forgotten to tell his ex-wife. "Come back in fifteen minutes, and I'll have something ready." If the woman said thanks, Cary didn't hear her.

Cary braced her hands on the countertop. She pulled in a deep breath then let it out slowly. She'd thought Micah's kisses meant something. She'd been wrong. Even if he was hanging around Marlene because of Willa Wild, the last thing she needed was to get in the middle of quirky family dynamics.

The thought of Willa Wild gave Cary an idea. She'd make a lunch her little buddy would love. On the top shelf of the pantry she'd found a wicker picnic basket. She cut watermelon and cantaloupe into balls and added cherries. Slipping fried chicken left over from the night before into a large bag, she tucked it into the basket along with the fruit salad. Into a plastic bowl, she scooped several servings of potato salad. This wasn't a fancy feast, but it was perfect picnic food.

Now for dessert. She pulled the stool into the pantry and found the Oreos Micah had hidden. She packed them on top so the little girl would be sure to see them. Nothing was too good for Willa Wild, and if it made Micah mad, so much the better.

Marlene was back in fifteen minutes for the food. She picked up the bag and left without a word. Cary watched out the kitchen window as Micah lifted Willa Wild into the truck and fastened her seat belt. He stepped back and held the door for Marlene. Cary could see him nod to the redhead before closing the door. Marlene's laugh carried into the kitchen, but it was Micah's smile when he looked at his ex-wife that hurt the most.

If it weren't for her fear of Mad Dog, she'd be out of here. Did she dare call Pansy again and see how things were going at home, maybe get some money? It had only been a couple of weeks since she left home. Even Mad Dog, big man that he thought he was, couldn't trace a call. If she kept it short...

Cary pulled her cell out of her pocket and turned the thing on. She'd purposely left it off. She scrolled down to see she had one new voice mail. After putting in her pin, she listened.

Pansy's voice came through but her words were garbled. *Hope you're fine* came through clear and *do you know*. Do I know what? She listened several times, but the words after were unintelligible. From what Cary could make out, Pansy didn't sound panicked, just curious and a little worried.

As the phone rang, Cary almost hung up three times. Was this a big mistake, or was she being paranoid?

"Oh my god, Cary. Are you all right?" Pansy talked a mile a minute and her words now came faster than usual. "Tell me you're all right. I've been so worried. I tried to call and even left you a message, but then I thought maybe I shouldn't, so I didn't call again."

"Pansy. Stop talking." She'd needed to talk to a friend. How the magpie chatter of her best friend could be calming, she didn't know, but it was. "Are you okay?"

"I'm okay. I'm not the one who ran away from the bad guys. Tell me you're safe."

Cary heard the crinkle of paper on the other end of the line. That would be Pansy was eating Twinkies. The woman lived on them. "I'm fine."

"Don't tell me where you are."

"I won't. Have you seen Mad Dog or any of his minions?" Cary sank into the lawn chair and put her feet on the porch rail.

More crinkling then Pansy spoke. "He's stopped by the

restaurant a couple of times and asked to speak to me. He's acted nice. Said you'd been dating, and he couldn't get ahold of you. He said he was worried because he hadn't heard from you. Like I'm going to believe that. Are you really okay?"

Cary smiled. If she had to have only one person in the world on her side, she'd choose Pansy. Pansy's appearance threw people off. They thought of her as a ditz, but Cary knew she was wicked smart and brave. "I'm fine. Mad Dog won't be able to find me here. It's so good to hear a friendly voice."

"Oh, honey. You call me any time. But don't do it too often. I think he's watching me. I've caught sight of a big guy following me a couple of times."

"I was going to ask you to withdraw some money from my account, but we'd better wait. I have to go now. Thanks, Pansy." Given a choice, she'd have stayed on the line with Pansy all day, but she had to be careful. No sense tempting fate.

Every bit of energy drained out of Cary's body, and she yearned for a nap. All she wanted was a life without hassle, but the drama dragon stalked her. She stood and reached for the sky, stretching her tired muscles. Instead of a nap, she'd take a walk. There was nothing like a little exercise to make a girl feel better—exercise and a giant bowl of chocolate.

She walked to the barn, stopping at the pen with the calves. Their rate of growth astounded her. Each one ran and played like any small child. When they saw her they bawled, demanding milk.

"You know it's not feeding time. Too much milk will give you a tummy ache. Willa Wild told me, and Willa Wild knows calves." As she poked her fingers through into the pen, the smaller calf latched on. "You're little, but you're mighty aren't you?"

She hadn't been on the ranch long, but she already knew this was the type of place she wanted to stay. Not the Circle W. It had one too many women as it was, but something similar.

A movement at the end of the barn caught her attention. Clinton Barnes came through the door, a smile on his face. "Hey, Miss Cary. Come out here to visit with the babies?"

"I have a while before I need to start dinner. You're back early." She'd been drawn to Clint from the first time she'd seen him. He was kind and acted like she belonged here.

"I gotta ask you a question." Clint picked up a piece of straw and split it in half then leaned against the stall door.

"What have I done wrong now?"

"Done wrong? Nothin' that I know of. Come with me." When they reached the barnyard, he turned toward the creek. "Been down here?"

She shook her head no then followed him down the gentle hill. Giant cottonwood trees towered over the creek and threw shadowed stripes across the water. A gentle wind ruffled the leaves and grass. Clint stopped by the edge then climbed out onto a huge branch that hung over the water. He held out his hand.

Cary slid onto the rough bark and dangled her feet over the creek. She was coming back here by herself soon. It was a beautiful spot and quiet, soothing. "You wanted to ask me something?"

Clint leaned back and looked up into the tree branches. "You said something to Micah about me and Millie." He kept his gaze averted, seemingly engrossed in the sight of the trees.

"I might have. Are you mad?" She'd done it again.

Always sticking her nose in everybody's business whether or not they wanted her advice.

He pulled out a pocketknife and cleaned his fingernails. When he raised his gaze to hers, she could swear it was filled with sadness. "Not mad."

They sat in silence until Cary was fidgeting with tension. Had she really overstepped her bounds? To curb her impatience she watched the water ripple underneath their feet.

"If you tell anyone this, I'll deny it." His expression changed from sadness to determination when his gaze locked with hers.

"I won't."

"Millie is special, but she's fixated on Micah. No use for me to step in between."

"He's stringing her along?" One more black mark penciled in beside Micah's name in her book.

"No, Micah wouldn't do that. He just doesn't see the truth." Clint helped her off the tree trunk, and they started back to the house.

"Someone should tell her." Cary turned to Clint and put her hand on his arm. "Do you want me to talk to her?"

"No!" He stopped, caught himself then continued. "Promise me you won't say anything to Millie or Micah."

## 10

The five short miles to the lake, stuck in the truck cab with Marlene, felt a miserable as calving in knee deep snow. The picnic would only last a few hours, but even a minute spent with his ex-wife was too long. After helping his daughter out of the truck, he grabbed the picnic lunch Marlene had packed.

The fact that his ex-wife had taken the time to fix food surprised him. Usually, she didn't bother. He had an uneasy feeling about this whole family day, but his daughter was so excited he wouldn't put a damper on it.

"Willa, you stay away from the water. It's too cold." Marlene followed the girl to the sandy area and spread out a quilt.

Willa had started down to the water's edge but turned back when Marlene spoke. "Aw, mom. I want to go wading."

"Come here, shortcake." Micah leaned into the back of the pickup and lifted out a fishing pole. "How about some fishing?"

Willa whooped in delight and did a cartwheel in the sand before running to his side. Together, they put a worm on the hook then Micah walked his daughter to the edge of the lake and stood by while she tried to cast.

"Want me to help you?" This little girl was everything to him, and she was growing up too fast.

"I can do it!" She bit on her lower lip and cast again. This time she got the hook out into the water. "See!"

Micah walked back a few feet and sat in the sand. The day was perfect, or would have been if Cary had been here instead of Marlene.

Marlene stood beside him and smiled down. "How do you like my suit?"

Think of the devil, and she will appear. He continued to watch his daughter and repeated the mantra that got him through Marlene's visits. *Having Willa Wild was worth anything his ex-wife could throw at him.*

She took the edges of what looked like a big, blue silk scarf and untied the knot at her hip. The bikini underneath was smaller than a Sunday handkerchief.

Marlene spread the scarf on the ground and lowered herself down beside Micah. "Well? Do you like it?"

"Sure." He stood to walk away when she latched on to his pant leg. He'd tried every way outside of coming right out and saying he didn't want her to touch him. It appeared he'd have to be blunt.

"Stay for a minute. I have something I want to say to you." Marlene stood and shaded her eyes with one hand. "Willa, come over here."

The little girl ignored her, but Micah knew she'd heard. Sometimes Willa was an obstinate little thing.

When her daughter continued to ignore her, Marlene laughed. "Willa, you're going to want to hear this."

Micah had a bad feeling in his gut. Marlene was up to

something. She'd been sneaky in the past, and he'd never liked her surprises.

Marlene knelt down beside her daughter. She took the little girl's face in her hands and gave her a quick kiss. "Let me whisper in your ear."

Willa's blue eyes went wide. She dropped the fishing pole and bounced with excitement. "Can I tell Pa now?" With Marlene's nod, Willa turned to Micah. "Mom is coming home to stay. We'll be a family like the other kids at school."

Micah's heart sank. Was there no end to Marlene's deceitfulness? Now she was dragging their little girl into her plans.

"Isn't that great, Pa?" Willa stood before him, her face lit with joy. "Mom says she's going to stay forever."

Micah put his hand on Willa Wild's shoulder. "Why don't you go catch us a fish for supper. We'll talk about this when we get home."

Willa ran to where she'd laid the fishing pole and resumed her fishing.

Micah rounded on Marlene, being careful to keep his voice low so his daughter wouldn't hear him explode. "What the hell is this?" It was all he could do to look at her. At one time, he'd thought she was the most beautiful woman in the world, but her deceiving ways had shown him true beauty wasn't on the outside of a person.

"Now, Micah. Calm down." Marlene placed her hand on his chest and gave him the smile that had worked until the day he found out it didn't mean a thing. "I thought it was time I came home. Willa needs her mother."

"All these years she didn't need you. Is that what you're saying?" His voice rose, and Willa turned to look at them. Micah waved and forced a smile. "Any luck?"

"Nothing yet, Pa."

"The Circle W isn't your home any more. You gave up that right when you left us. You don't get it back."

"But Micah, I want to come home." Tears filled her large blue eyes, and just as if she'd choreographed it, one rolled down her cheek.

Too bad she didn't work as hard at becoming an actress as she did at manipulating people. The way she could turn emotions off and on would have earned her an Oscar. But Micah had been through this enough times to know when she was bluffing. "You're not going to live with us."

Marlene's expression turned from heartbroken to irate with a bunch of determined thrown in to spare. "You, not me but you, will break your daughter's heart if you make me leave. She wants me here."

"I don't want you here."

"This is more important than your feelings. Willa needs a mother, and I'm it." She bent and picked up the scarf with a flourish and started for the truck. "Willa, come see what I fixed for lunch."

Micah watched as Marlene walked away, her hips swaying. She looked over her shoulder and gave him a look that said she was in control. The only way to stop her was to break his daughter's heart, and he wasn't sure he could do that.

Willa Wild ran to her mother and took what looked like a chicken leg. "Yay, Cary's chicken."

So Marlene hadn't packed the lunch. She'd gotten Cary to do it. And she'd said she made it. Another small lie to get what she wanted.

Willa Wild called to him. "Pa, come eat. We've got Oreos for dessert."

A smile broke out on his face. Cary knew he was hiding

the Oreos to keep Willa from eating them all. She'd made the lunch her own no matter what Marlene said.

Marlene put her arms around her daughter. "I love you, baby girl. I'm so glad I'm going to be back home."

"Love you, too, Mama." A mouthful of chicken muffled the girl's words.

"Micah, do you want potato salad with your chicken?" Marlene's smug look told him she was sure she'd won this battle.

He could play the game, but he wouldn't use Willa Wild as a pawn. "Yes, please." He took the seat farthest from Marlene and relaxed. For the moment, he'd enjoy Cary's chicken and a day with his daughter.

Marlene glanced up from her plate of food. "Willa thinks I should take the room next to hers."

For a moment he thought he saw a flash of fear roll across Marlene's face, but it disappeared as fast as it came. "We'll talk about it when we get home, Marlene."

"For Willa's sake," Marlene said. "Think of your daughter."

"Unlike you, I always think of my daughter." He turned away and walked to the water's edge, bending to grab the fishing pole. He reeled in the line then stowed it in the back of the pickup. "Come on. Time to get back."

"Aw, Pa." Willa Wild ran to him. "I didn't get to catch a fish."

He reached out and pushed the curly, red strand that had come loose from her braid behind her ear. His little girl had it all. Her mother's beauty, but more importantly, she was kind and sweet. Could he keep her from becoming manipulative like Marlene? Yes, or die trying.

"Micah, would you come help me pack up?" Marlene stood before the remnants of the lunch.

How hard could it be to put the food in the bag and fold the quilt? With a sigh, he walked back to his ex-wife.

She put her arms around his neck and pressed her body against his.

Micah pushed her away. "Don't touch me again. We're divorced, and I'm not taking you back."

"Oh, you'll let me come back." The determined look on her face turned his stomach. "If you fight me on this, I'll tell Willa you're forcing me to leave. She'll hate you."

THE LOOK her ex-husband gave Marlene should have burned her to ashes. He hated her. Did he really think she'd stay if she had anywhere else to go? The ranch was dirty, boring, filled with work, and entirely too far from the excitement of a big city.

She bent down and grabbed the edge of the red, white and pink quilt. Micah's grandmother probably made it. The old woman could do just about anything. She'd tried to teach Marlene to cook and sew the first few months they'd been married, but she couldn't get through to Gram she didn't want to do that crap. She'd married Micah because he had money.

Oh, she'd thought she loved him. She wasn't mercenary, but she also knew life only gave you what you chose to take.

Marlene shook the blanket and folded it into a messy square and marched toward the truck. This day hadn't turned out the way she'd planned, but it would do. Micah wouldn't dare kick her out. He was too afraid of breaking Willa Wild's heart.

Having his parents die when he was young had messed with his mind and made it easier for her to get her way. She didn't have much love left for Micah, but there was one thing she thanked Micah for every day. He was a great father for their Willa.

She lifted her daughter into the pickup and fastened her seatbelt. She loved this little girl more than anything or anybody on this earth. She just couldn't live her life on this ranch. There were big things out there waiting for Marlene, and as soon as she got on her feet, she was going looking.

"Willa Wild, what do you think of driving into town and catching a movie with me and Pa?" God, she hated that name. Sounded like a hick, but she knew it would bother him that she used it. She watched as Micah's knuckles turned white as he gripped the steering wheel.

Willa seemed to know not to push. "What do you think, Pa?"

Micah's chest swelled as he pulled in a huge breath and held it for a moment. He didn't answer until he'd let it out slowly. "Not today, Willa. We've got chores to do at home."

"Really, Micah. You never let our daughter have any fun." Again, she'd pushed too hard, but one of the few pleasures in this god forsaken area was getting Micah all riled up. From the look on his face, she'd riled him to the max.

He turned his head until he looked her in the eyes. "No."

There'd been a time she could get this man to do anything she wanted. But that had been gone for a while. He tolerated her while staying as far away from her as he could. If she weren't careful, he might cut her loose.

She smiled. Time to play the game smart. "You're right. We'll go to a movie another day."

Marlene tried to make small talk on the drive home, but Willa was the only one answering her questions.

Micah pretended to focus on keeping the truck on the road. When she asked him a direct question, he acted like he was stone deaf. But she knew him. He couldn't stay mad long, and if she continued to be nice, he'd give in. There wasn't a mean bone in Micah's body and he'd do anything to keep Willa happy.

And if her mama stayed, Willa would be happy.

THE SOUND of happy chatter let Cary know the family was home from their day at the lake. She hurried toward the stairs in an attempt to escape to her room. The last thing she wanted was to watch Marlene gloat.

"Cary, Cary, wait up." Willa Wild's voice called to her, and no matter how much she wanted to avoid Micah and Marlene, she couldn't ignore her young friend.

She stopped and sat on the stairs. "What's up, Little Willa?"

The tiny redhead scrambled up to the step beside Cary and plopped down. "We did lots of fun things today. Guess."

"I have to guess?" Cary pulled the child on to her lap. When the little girl nodded, she held up one finger. "You ate lunch at the lake?"

Willa giggled, her high-pitched laugh sent waves of happiness through Cary. "Of course. You packed the lunch. What else?"

"How did you know that?"

"It was your chicken." Willa Wild slipped her small hand into Cary's.

"Okay, second. You went swimming?" Cary touched Willa Wild's nose with her finger.

"Pa said it was too cold." Willa crawled off her lap then danced up and down the stairs in excitement. "But he taught me to fish."

Cary rounded her eyes in a good imitation of wonder and gasped. "Did you catch one?"

The little girl stopped, and the excitement drained from her expression. Her shoulders slumped, and she dropped down at Cary's feet. "No. I tried and tried, but not one of those fishes would bite the worm. I really wanted to eat fish for dinner."

Cary stood and took Willa Wild's hand. "Maybe next time, honey."

Willa's face lit with a smile. "And I gots another surprise. My mama is staying this time. She's gonna live with us."

Cary felt a jab of disappointment. Disappointment gave way to disillusionment, although she didn't have a right to feel that emotion either. She was just an employee who the boss had kissed.

Willa was giving her a confused look.

"That's exciting. You and your daddy will like that, won't you?" Cary started up the stairs then looked over her shoulder. "I've got something to do right now. I'll be down to get dinner ready in a few minutes."

She could feel the girl watching her as she mounted the stairs, and she hurried to her room and closed the door. Could her life get any worse? Flinging herself onto the bed, she covered her eyes with her hands. Well, if Mad Dog caught her it would be much worse, but still . . .

She sat up and leaned back against the gray tufted headboard, folding her hands behind her head and crossing her legs on the comforter. Light filtered in through the plantation shutters while she focused her attention on the photo on the wall. Micah as a child with his grandparents. Even though he'd lost his parents, he'd had people who cared.

A life without drama. That had been her goal for a while now, and she was sure she couldn't find it here. In a few more days it would be two weeks since she'd arrived. The paycheck she'd get would give her enough money to head for New York. If she slept in the car and didn't eat too much, it was enough to hold her over until she could find another job.

The soft tap, tap, tap of someone knocking on her door drew her attention. She opened the door to find Willa Wild on the other side. "Hi, honey. Did you need something?"

Willa nodded. Cary stepped back then followed the girl into the room. Willa shut the door then looked at Cary.

"What's wrong?" The expression on Willa's face broke Cary's heart. This child didn't deserve to be sad. Cary sat on the bed then drew Willa onto her lap.

"Pa's not happy about Mama staying." Willa's fingers slipped through Cary's, and she laid her head on Cary's shoulder. "I don't think Mama's happy about it either. I don't know what to do."

Cary put her hand on Willa's head and cradled her. The tiny body shuddered with a huge sigh. How had she found herself in the middle of this family dispute? And what could she say to this child that wouldn't hurt her more? "It's not your job to make them happy. Your job is to be kind and smart and as happy as you can be. They will work out the rest by themselves."

Willa Wild gave her a tremulous grin, her lower lip quivering. "How do I do that?"

Cary laughed as she hugged Willa. "Honey, if I knew that, I'd—" What would she do? She'd decide what she wanted out of life and go after it. "Come on. Let's go get dinner on the table before Barnsey chews us out for being late."

She took Willa's hand, and they skipped down the stairs. As they entered the kitchen, Marlene came through the back door, her frown conveying her mood. When she saw them, the woman pasted a wide, fake smile on her face. "Did Willa tell you our big news?"

About a dozen sarcastic remarks were on the tip of Cary's tongue, but no matter how much she disliked Marlene, she wasn't about to draw Willa into this mess. "She did. It will be so nice for her to have you around all the time." She tousled the messy red hair and smiled at Willa. The worried look on the child's face told her she'd done the right thing.

"Baby girl, will you go get my purse? I think it's in the living room." Marlene watched her daughter leave the room then rounded on Cary. "You stay away from Micah. He might not be as happy as he could be about me being back, but he'll change his mind when he sees how happy his daughter is."

The venom in the woman's voice caused Cary to take a step back. "I'm not—"

"I know your type. Be warned."

## 11

Usually the calm quiet atmosphere of the barn settled Micah's mind and gave him the peace to work out his problems. This afternoon, it only gave him time to get angrier. Marlene had stooped to a new low using their daughter to try to wheedle her way back onto the ranch.

Although he'd do anything to keep Willa Wild happy, even if he let Marlene come back, she'd leave again—and break Willa's heart all over. It was time to take control of the situation and quit letting Marlene call the shots.

He stood and dusted off his jeans. Putting off the confrontation hadn't accomplished anything so far, and the battle wasn't over yet. He felt like a child dragging his feet over a chore he didn't want to do.

As he mounted the back steps, he heard Marlene's voice, her words just soft enough so he couldn't make them out. Stepping into the kitchen, he found Cary and Marlene standing face to face.

Marlene turned and when she saw him, she smiled. "Hi,

baby. I was just telling Cary our good news." She hurried over to him and put her arm through his.

"Marlene, come take a walk with me." He raised his gaze to Cary's. "Would you keep Willa Wild in here for a while?"

When she nodded, he turned around and put his hand on Marlene's back, pushing her out the door a little bit harder than he'd intended.

"Micah, watch out." When Marlene stumbled, he took her arm and hurried her down the stairs.

He didn't speak as they crossed the barnyard, but Marlene kept up a running commentary of all the things she was going to do now that she was home. He pulled open the heavy barn door and followed his chattering ex-wife into the dim interior.

Light filtered in from the two windows set high in the walls, and dust floated in the air from the horse's movements in his stall. The sweet scent of hay filled the space.

"It stinks in here. Is there anything we can do to get rid of this odor?" Marlene turned to Micah, wrapping her arms around his neck. "Never mind, I can get used to it. After all, I won't be spending that much time out here."

The overwhelming desire to throttle this woman had him grinding his teeth. He took hold of her wrists and removed her hands. "You can't stay."

She reached up and stroked her fingers along his cheek. "Sure I can. I promise I won't leave this time. I'm ready to be your wife and Willa's mother." She'd stepped closer, deliberately rubbing her breasts against his chest.

There'd been a time when he couldn't have resisted her, a time when he'd forgiven her anything, but that time was gone. "Let me be clear. You have three days to find another place to live. After that, I'll pack your things and drop you off at the bus station."

Her arms dropped limp to her sides and her eyes filled with tears.

"Crying won't change my mind. Three days." It amazed him that he'd ever found this woman alluring.

The pitiful expression on her face morphed into anger. With the speed of a prizefighter, her hand snaked out, and she slapped his cheek. "Willa won't ever forgive you for forcing me to leave."

He folded his arms across his chest. His anger faded away as he watched her scramble for a way to win. "That's between me and Willa. It has nothing to do with you."

Her jaw set and a mulish look transformed her face. "She'll believe me when I tell her you forced me to go so you can have your girlfriend." Her breath came in short spurts and red blotches covered her once lovely face.

He met her angry glare and held it until she looked away. "I don't believe you will intentionally hurt our daughter, and you know if you tell her that, she'll be torn between us."

"Micah, please."

"Three days." He walked half way to the door then turned back. "If you need help moving, Clint is available."

He heard her soft sobs. He'd heard them before, but he'd hardened his heart to her wiles. The sun was brighter and warmer when he stepped through the door. He wasn't kidding himself for a second that Marlene would give up. He knew they had at least a couple more confrontations before she realized he meant what he'd said.

When he entered the back door, Willa Wild stood on the step stool, the apron Cary had tied around her waist hanging to her toes. A white splash of flour spread down the side of her cheek and across the counter.

"Pa, I'm making cupcakes. Cary teached me."

Cary, covered with an equal amount of flour, grinned. "She's a natural."

The sight of this woman with his child made his chest clench. He knew Marlene loved Willa, just not as much as she loved herself. While Cary had only known Willa for a couple of weeks, she seemed to really treasure the time they spent together.

He took his finger and brushed some of the flour from Willa's face. "What kind are you making?"

"Fairy cupcakes. They got magic in 'em." Excitement colored Willa Wild's cheeks pink and deepened the blue of her eyes. "I'm making one special for you and Mama."

And all the happiness he'd found while watching these two hit the floor like a drunk at Mardi Gras. "Willa, I need to talk to you about that."

She turned her elfin face to his, her expression all knowing. "In a minute, Pa. I have to finish the cupcakes first."

Cary brushed off her hands then wiped them on one of his grandmother's embroidered hand towels. "Willa, you keep stirring. I need to talk to your father for just a moment. Okay?"

The little girl stirred the thick batter with all the strength her skinny arms could manage. She grinned at Cary then Micah. "I'm gonna be a great cook, just like Cary."

Cary led him into the living room and out onto the porch. She leaned against the porch rail and raised her rich brown eyes to his. "You know Willa Wild is worried about you and Marlene?"

He sat on the rail next to her. When his arm brushed hers, she moved a few inches away. "Damn! I'd hoped she hadn't picked up on that. Marlene broke the news in front of her hoping I would give in. Not this time. I gave her three days to find another place to live."

Cary bit her bottom lip. "What are you going to tell Willa?"

"The truth." He stood and walked to the other end of the porch and stood looking out over the pasture. With a short nod, he turned back to Cary. "I can't keep letting Marlene breeze in and out of our lives. She's promised to stay this time, but I can already see her getting restless."

"Willa sees more than you know. She'll understand. She might not like it, but she'll understand." Cary lifted up and gave him a kiss on the cheek. "You're a good man."

Micah wrapped his hand around her upper arm and pulled her close. Before she could object, he lowered his lips to hers. Fire raced through his body. Lightning raced through his brain. Even when he was enamored with Marlene in the early days of their relationship, he hadn't felt like this. An overwhelming sense of peace was present whenever he was with Cary.

He raised his head and looked into her eyes, trying to convey his feelings. He pulled her close and held her against his body absorbing the warmth she gave him.

Cary was good for him, and she was good for his daughter. As soon as he got things under control with Marlene, he'd tell Cary how he felt about her.

As they stood there, he heard the scrape of a shoe on the stones of the walkway. Then Marlene cleared her throat.

Cary jumped and tried to pull away, but he kept his arms around her. He looked at his ex-wife. "You need something?"

CARY ALWAYS THOUGHT of herself as pretty strong-minded, but being in the vicinity of Micah West was proving her wrong. No matter how determined she was to stay an arm's length away from him, when his lips touched hers, she melted into a gooey puddle. The only option, she realized, was to leave sooner rather than later.

With a paycheck for two weeks work in her pocket, she had enough money to go somewhere where Micah wasn't. She'd planned on working at least another week, but that was out of the question. Marlene wasn't leaving soon enough. And Cary couldn't stay with the woman here.

But then there was Willa Wild. She'd miss the little girl with all her heart. Willa was the daughter she'd probably never have. She pulled two hash brown and egg casseroles out of the oven and placed them on the table, sticking a large spoon into each one. Life with Willa Wild and Micah wasn't in the cards.

She'd carried most of her things to the car the night before when the house had been asleep, and she was going to make her escape after she'd served breakfast. With a roast in the crockpot and lasagna in the fridge ready to be baked, the men would have food for today.

Cary picked up the puppy and clutched him to her chest. She scratched at the soft fluff behind his ears while he licked her cheek. "I'd love to take you with me, but it wouldn't be right. There's no place in the city for a ranch dog. You'll take good care of Willa Wild for me, won't you, Goodun."

"Hey, Miss Cary." As Clint came through the back door, his customary smile on his face, she straightened. "How's your day going?"

She'd miss this man, too. He'd become a friend. Silly as it sounded, he'd helped her learn what she needed to survive out here. "Just dandy."

He put his arm around her shoulder and gave her a squeeze. "It's lots nicer with you here." Grabbing the largest plate, he filled it to overflowing then dumped catsup a half-inch thick over everything.

Turning away, she bit her lip to keep the tears from falling. She'd miss all these people. In such a short time, they'd become like family. But she'd lost other people she'd cared about, and she'd survived.

"I'm going into town. You need anything?" Clinton slicked up the last bit of eggs with his toast then put his plate in the sink.

With her emotions under control for now, she turned and gave him a big smile. "I need you to tell Millie how you feel."

Clint stared into the sink. "Nothin' to say."

"Poultry."

His brows drew together. "What?" He managed the question around a mouthful of food.

"It's from an old movie. Poultry is another word for chicken."

His bark of laughter brought a smile to her face. Grinning as he chewed, he nodded in agreement.

Cary patted his shoulder then hurried up the stairs. She was pretty sure she'd packed everything except her purse and phone, but she checked the closet and beneath the bed just to be sure. Hurrying out to the car, she tossed her bag into the back seat. If the good luck gods were on her side today, she'd be gone before anyone noticed.

Climbing into the shabby green Ford, she reached up and adjusted her rearview mirror. A movement in the mirror caught her eye.

Marlene hurried down the steps, both hands waving frantically.

With a sigh of resignation, Cary waited for the redhead to shimmy up to the driver's side. One good thing. This would be the last time she'd have to fake a pleasant expression for the woman.

"Can you give me a ride into town? Please."

What the hell was up with Marlene now? There was something definitely wrong when this woman acted nice. Cary wasn't making the return trip, so if she took Marlene, the woman would be stranded in town. "I'm going to visit a friend, so I won't be back out here until tomorrow. You won't have a way back to the ranch."

"That's okay. Micah will come get me." Marlene climbed into the passenger seat and buckled her seatbelt. "Let's go."

On a normal day, the drive to town took a little over fifteen minutes. Having Marlene in the car took normal out of the equation. The trip seemed never ending with Marlene's constant chatter about moving back to the ranch.

Leaving was the right decision. No matter how much the ranch felt like a home, Cary couldn't stay.

Rounding a curve halfway to town, Cary hit the brakes and narrowly missed the car sitting sideways in the middle of the road.

The man in a white suit stood by the open hood. He turned and rushed to the driver's side. "Hey, can you help us?" He gestured to the car, and Cary could see another person sitting in the passenger seat.

"What's wrong?" Cary called to him. She opened her door and started to climb out, but thought better of that. Her Spidey sense had alarm bells clanging in her brain. If these guys had car trouble, why was it sitting crossways, nearly blocking the road? She didn't recognize the man, but there were many people from this area she hadn't met yet. "Marlene . . ."

"Let me do the talking." Marlene turned and opened her door but didn't get out. "I can handle these guys."

A shiver ran down Cary's back. Was something wrong, or was she being paranoid? Marlene didn't seem bothered. Cary started to follow Marlene, but stopped when the second man climbed out.

He was even bigger than the first with a triple chin and rolls of fat around his middle. For a man of his size, he reached the front of Cary's car before either of the women could react. He effortlessly lifted Marlene out of the car and held her by her upper arms high enough so only her toes touched the ground.

Marlene struggled but couldn't break free.

Cary froze.

"Climb out of the car." White Suit leaned toward her window his hand on the door handle. "If you don't want that pretty little girl to disappear, you'll do as I say."

Her heartbeats thundered in her ears as adrenaline raced through her veins. Disbelief warred with panic in her brain. They didn't have Willa Wild. They couldn't. She'd stayed at her friend's family in town last night. They had to be bluffing. "I don't believe you. You don't have her."

The thug jerked the door open and took a step back. He held out his hand as if he were Prince Charming bent on helping her out of the car.

Her instincts screamed to get away, but as she didn't have any choice at the moment, she climbed out.

White Suit leaned closer, and she couldn't stop herself from moving away from him. Were these Mad Dog's men? They had to be. They'd found her, and she'd endangered Willa Wild by staying too long. Just the thought of Micah's daughter being hurt made her head spin.

The smaller man pulled a phone out of his pocket and brought up a picture. There, on screen, was Willa Wild holding a puppy. Triple Chins knelt behind her, his bulk dwarfing her tiny frame. Cary's legs gave out at the knowledge these men had Willa. As she hit the ground, the gravel dug into her skin, but she didn't notice.

She grabbed the edge of the car door. It took all her concentration to keep her voice steady. "Let her go. Take me. I'll do whatever you want." Cary sucked in a lungful of air then another one. She had to get herself under control if she was to have any chance to help the little girl.

The man nearest to her smiled, showing his tobacco stained teeth. "That's a mighty nice offer, Marlene." He grabbed her arm and pulled her to her feet. "I think me and BJ can work with that."

"Wait. What?" She jerked her arm loose and stepped away. "I'm not Marlene. Did Mad Dog send you?"

Both sets of eyes stared at her then shifted in tandem to Marlene.

"You've got the wrong person," the redhead said, holding her hands up, backing away. The moment the men took a step toward her, she turned and ran.

As the thugs hurried after Marlene, Cary jumped into the Fiesta and turned the key. She shoved it into gear the same moment one of the men jerked the passenger door open. With the gas pedal to the floor, she barely missed the car in front of her. The little Ford fishtailed in the gravel before grabbing onto the asphalt.

Cary swerved the car down the narrow road. The bad guy kicked his feet, trying to gain a foothold while the door hinges shrieked in protest from his weight. Slamming on the brakes, she locked up the wheels before she stomped on the gas again. The door swung shut, pinning the man for a moment before he screamed and fell away.

She couldn't be over five miles from town. Five miles

that seemed to take five years. Willa Wild must be so frightened. Who knew where they'd hidden the little girl.

She rounded the last curve, and East Hope came into view. For once, there wasn't a living soul on Main Street. Panic made her misjudge her stopping distance, and her bumper dented the light post in front of the jail. The car hadn't come to a complete stop before she bailed out and ran to the door of the sheriff's office.

"They've got Willa," she cried, but the silence told her no one was in the room. Turning, she ran to the café. That was the most likely place to find help.

She raced down the cracked sidewalk and hit the restaurant door at a full run. It banged against the wall as she threw it open, the bell clanging. "Help, they've got Willa!"

The din of numerous conversations fell silent. Every head in the room turned toward her. Micah stood from the booth where he sat with Clint and hurried across the room. "Calm down. What's going on?"

Cary grabbed his shirtsleeves, frantically tugging him toward the door. "Some men stopped us. They've got Willa. We've got to hurry." The last word came out on a sob.

Micah took her hands and pulled her to him. "No one has Willa. She's right here with us." He pointed to the booth. At the sight of the little girl, her bright red hair curling around her face, her brows knit into a frown waving one small hand sent a shock of relief racing down her limbs. She locked her knees and turned to Micah. "But they've got—

A child's wail filled the room. "They've got Goodun."

## 12

Micah's heart had stopped when Cary came through the door, her face ashen and her expression wild. He pulled out a chair and lowered her into it before kneeling down. "Start from the beginning. What happened when you left the ranch?"

Cary gasped and tried to talk but she was shaking so hard, the words were unintelligible.

Micah rubbed his thumbs across the back of her hands, his voice soothing. "Try again, and take your time."

"We were driving into town when we saw a car stopped in the middle of the road." Cary rubbed her face with her hands then raised her gaze to his. "Two men. They had a picture on their phone of Willa Wild standing with them. They said they had her. God, I was so scared."

When Cary stood and began pacing, Micah drew her into his arms. "She's safe and so are you."

Cary melted against him. "I thought it was Mad Dog. That he'd sent his men after me, but they wanted Marlene."

Micah leaned back. "Who's Mad Dog, and where's Marlene?"

Her voice rose to an almost wail. "I don't know! Oh, god. I left her out there."

"And Mad Dog?" There was someone after Cary who would hurt Willa? What the hell was going on?

"I'll tell you all about it, but we need to help Marlene." The pleading look in her eyes convinced him to drop the subject for now. He scanned the room. "Hank, come with me. Cal, find the sheriff and send him out Hwy 21."

The three of them jumped into Micah's truck. As they left town, he noticed two more cars following. Apparently every man in the café was coming along. Leave it to the residents of East Hope to join in the battle.

With Cary pointing the way, Micah and the crew made it to the two men's car in no time flat. There was no sign of Marlene or either of her attackers.

Micah bailed out of his truck. Cary climbed out right behind him, placed her hands on his waist and peered around his shoulder. "Marlene," he yelled as he ran in the direction Cary pointed. "Marlene!"

He stopped for a second then heard a voice in the distance. He turned to Cary. "Stay in the truck."

"Not on your life," Cary said. "I'm staying with you."

He could either waste time arguing with her or find his ex-wife. He chose the latter. Climbing through a ravine and over a hill, he finally saw someone in the distance. As he drew closer, he saw Marlene holding a gun in one hand and a large branch in the other. One of the crooks sat on the ground in front of her, blood dripping from a gash on his forehead, and the other stood back, his hands raised in surrender.

Marlene flashed him a smile as he approached. "'Bout time you got here."

Hank lumbered up, followed by the rest of the townspeople. In no time at all, they had the two men trussed up like roping calves. Townspeople surrounded Marlene as she told them the story of how she'd beaten the men who tried to kidnap her.

Micah looked around in time to see Cary walk back to the truck.

When he was sure the situation was under control, he made his way back to Cary.

She sat in the truck cab, alone, her head in her hands. "They didn't have Willa, but they could have." A tear ran down her cheek, and she swiped at it with her hand. She didn't look at him as she spoke. "If it had been Mad Dog, he would have had her."

Anger welled up in Micah as he thought of what could have happened. "Who the hell is Mad Dog?" Had she purposely led bad people to his town, to his ranch?

She raised her gaze to his, her eyes red rimmed, her jaw clenched. "My lousy, stupid ex-boyfriend owed him money. Mad Dog couldn't find him so he was going to take his revenge out of my hide if I didn't pay what was owed. When I didn't have it, the bum burned me with a cigar." She pulled up the sleeve of her T-shirt, revealing a large bandage.

The puckered skin turned his stomach, but he couldn't let Cary sway his thinking. "So you came here?"

"He told me he'd come back in a week. There was no way I could come up with that much money, so I ran."

Micah folded his arms over his chest. "He could have followed you here, right?"

"He was seen by a friend of mine in Salt Lake three days ago. I was leaving today. When these guys stopped us, I thought Mad Dog had found me. I'm so sorry."

Micah waited to see where she'd throw the blame.

Marlene had never taken responsibility for anything in her life, and he sure couldn't see her taking responsibility now.

Cary stood then looked him in the eyes. "I'm so sorry. I should never have come here in the first place. I'll go as soon as we get back to town."

Micah nodded to her then turned back to see about getting the men to the sheriff. His taste in women had to be the worst on record. Not one, but two women had dragged his family into their crooked schemes.

The thought of some evil person getting their hands on his daughter sent shivers down his spine. Just as they got the men to the trucks, Sheriff Madison pulled up, siren wailing, lights flashing. In minutes they were handcuffed and on their way back to town.

Cary stared at him for a moment before climbed in with Millie and Clint.

Marlene climbed into Micah's truck, excitement rolling off her in waves. "Did you see how I got them?" She turned, her eyes shining, her breath coming in short gasps.

Micah clenched his jaws to keep from turning on her with all the anger and fear that filled his body.

"What?" Marlene put her hand on his shoulder. "Everything turned out all right."

"What would have happened if they'd gotten their hands on Willa?" He was having a hard time keeping his voice below an all-out yell. "What then, Marlene?"

"I don't know what you're so all-fired mad about. They never had Willa. They just took a picture of her yesterday." Marlene slumped into the seat, building to a full on pout.

"To take that picture that man was within inches of her. He probably touched her. He could have grabbed her." He lost the battle to keep calm. "Marlene! What the fuck is wrong with you?"

She turned, the look on her face telling him she'd finally realized what could have happened. "Riley wouldn't have hurt her. He just sent the men to scare me."

"Even if you're right, and I'm not sure you are, has it occurred to you how scared our daughter would have been?"

Marlene wilted, but Micah didn't think she really got it. He didn't have time now to try to explain, and he wasn't sure she wanted to know. All he knew was he would do everything in his power to keep her away from his daughter from now on.

When they pulled up in front of the café, Willa and Clint stood waiting. He scooped his daughter into his arms and absorbed the wonderful scent of little girl. "Kiss your mother goodbye. We need to get home." He set her on the ground in front of Marlene, but didn't let go of her hand. He had to find some normalcy before he collapsed.

Willa Wild gave him a puzzled look. "Isn't Mama staying with us?"

Marlene leaned down and kissed her daughter. Micah was afraid she would make a fuss, but for once, she did the right thing. "No, baby. I have some things I have to do."

She kissed her mother then looked up at her father. "Is Cary coming back with us?"

How did he answer her? The two women who meant the most to his young daughter had betrayed them. "I think she has something else she has to do, too."

He'd just put his daughter in the truck and fastened her seat belt when the sheriff showed up. "Micah, I need to talk to you, and Marlene. Got a few minutes?"

"I'll take Willa Wild home," Clint said.

Micah nodded and followed the sheriff to his office, trailed by Marlene who stopped every few feet to talk to one person or another. Micah had the sneaking suspicion she was enjoying all the attention.

Cary stood in the corner of the sheriff's office, her shoulders slumped, her arms wrapped around her waist. She didn't look up as they entered.

When Marlene saw Cary, she reached out and put her hand through Micah's arm. Her body pressed against his, and she had the nerve to smile at Cary. "Are you all right, honey?"

Out of the corner of his eye, he saw Cary turn away without a word then his anger focused on the woman who had made his life miserable for more years than he wanted to count. "Get your god-damned hands off me!"

THE PURE ANGER in Micah's voice caused Cary's head to jerk around.

Marlene had backed away from her ex-husband, her face flushed. "Micah! Don't you swear at me. Willa might hear."

Even in this scary situation, his ex-wife was still trying to gain the advantage. Ignoring Marlene, he turned to the sheriff. "Sorry, Matt. What did you need?"

Cary looked from the sheriff to Micah and back. Although it would break her heart to leave this town and this man, she couldn't bear for him to look at her the way he did at Marlene.

Sheriff Madison turned to Cary. "I think we're done. You stay in town until I give you the go ahead to leave. Shouldn't be more than a day or two."

As she made her way to the door, she heard Marlene

begin to answer questions, her voice rising in excitement. She pulled the door shut with a click.

The day was as beautiful as a spring day could be. Sun shining, fluffy clouds in the sky and just enough of a breeze to keep it from being too hot. The way her heart was breaking, she'd have preferred dark clouds, lightning, and thunder.

Cary walked down the sidewalk to her car. What the hell was she going to do now? She couldn't leave, and she had no place to stay. Well, she'd slept in her car before, and it wouldn't kill her to do it again.

She'd asked the sheriff to check with the local police about Mad Dog, but didn't know why she bothered. The way her luck ran, he was probably on his way here now.

She fingered the check in her pocket. When Micah had paid his employees last night, the plan had been to cash the check on her way out of town. No time like the present, she thought as she walked to the bank.

She looked around for Mr. Loveland, but a young cashier was the only person present.

The woman counted out the bills with a smile. "Do you want to open an account?"

Cary stared at the pile of bills in her hand. That had been a dream she'd played with. Staying in East Hope and belonging to the town and Micah. That dream died as soon as Micah found out about Mad Dog. "No, thanks."

The young woman gave her a classic eye roll. "Mr. Loveland wants us to ask that of everyone. He's always looking for new accounts."

A genuine smile spread across Cary's face. Oh to be that innocent again.

"Thanks for using East Hope Bank. Please come in

again. "The pretty blonde gave her a conspiratorial smile. "He wants us to say that, too."

Cary waved goodbye then stepped onto the street. Her car sat in front of the sheriff's office where she'd left it on her panicked race into town. Afraid she'd run into Micah or Marlene, she decided to walk around town until they left.

"Cary!" Millie waved her hands as she raced across the street. Her carrot red bouffant tilted slightly to one side, and she was missing the bright red lipstick she was known for. "I've been looking all over for you."

Cary sucked in a deep breath. Millie's animosity was all she needed right now, but maybe the woman had been right to dislike her. She'd let everyone down. Managing what she hoped was a convincing smile she turned to the woman and waited for the attack.

Millie wrapped her arms around Cary and squeezed her tight.

What was going on here? Cary stiffened and it was all she could do to not pull away.

Millie held her at arms' length. "First of all, thank you for talking Clint into telling me how he felt. I feel so foolish for the way I've been acting."

What? When had this happened? "He talked to you?" Cary's life was falling apart, but here was one little ray of sunshine.

"Yep. He told me he thinks I'm special. All these years wasted because he didn't speak up, and I couldn't see a terrific man right in front of me." Millie put her arm around Cary's shoulders and gave her a gentle squeeze. "But back to you. Clint and I thought you might need a place to stay. I've got an extra room."

Millie had to be kidding, but when their eyes met, the woman seemed sincere.

Cary watched Millie as she spoke the embarrassing truth. "You do know I have someone after me, don't you? You might not want me anywhere around you."

Millie waved her hands, dismissing Cary's misgivings. "Just let that jerk show his face around here. He'll get a super-sized dose of western inhospitality."

The tears that she'd successfully balanced on her lower lashes broke free. She would have survived staying in her car, but the embarrassment of having the whole town know she had nowhere to go would have been humiliating. Now the woman who'd hated her when she'd arrived in East Hope was offering more than friendship. She was offering understanding and a place to stay. "Are you sure?"

Millie led Cary across the street. "We'll have fun. And if you think you want someone to talk to, you can tell me all your troubles."

"I'm afraid I'd scare you." Millie's caring attitude just made leaving harder. Maybe for a day, she could pretend she was here to stay.

"Honey, I'm a few years older than you. I bet I've been through anything you can tell me about and then some. Come on. Let's get you settled."

Millie stopped by Foodtown to give instructions to the cashier.

As she waited for new her friend in front of the grocery, Cary saw Micah and Marlene leaving the sheriff's office. Her strategy had been to sneak out of sight. This was about as unsneaky as a person could get.

Micah kept saying he didn't have feelings for Marlene, but every time Cary turned around, they were together. Without looking back, she followed Millie into the store, pretending she hadn't seen a thing.

Several times during the next two days, Cary was

called into the sheriff's office for questioning. By the morning of the third day she was free to go. Her grandfather had told her often enough about the silver lining in every dark cloud, and even in this heart-wrenching situation it was true. When Sheriff Madison told her Mad Dog was dead, she felt equal measures of relief and pity. The man had been scum, but she'd never wished for that.

Just a few days after she'd fled from Denver, he'd tried to strong-arm another woman. Apparently he'd picked the wrong victim, because she'd put one round right through his heart. Must have been a great shot, because Mad Dog's heart was no bigger than a pea.

"Can't I talk you into staying? You belong here." Millie stood in the doorway to the bedroom, her hands in the pockets of her jeans. "You don't have to work for Micah. I could hire you."

Cary folded and packed the few clothes she'd brought with her. She turned to her friend. "I appreciate your offer. You'll never know how much your kindness means to me, but I have to go back. Now that Mad Dog isn't a problem, I have to return my friend's car and take care of some business."

Millie crossed the room and pulled Cary into a hug, the scent of her ever-present Tabu perfume enveloping Cary in warmth. When Millie stepped back, she said, "Will you come back?"

No, she wouldn't be coming back. Although she'd miss Millie and Clint and the other East Hopeians, she couldn't bear having Micah hate her. "Probably not. Please understand. Maybe you can come visit me."

Millie walked with her as she carried her duffel bag to the car.

After popping the trunk, she tossed the bag in then gave Millie a hug. "I'll miss you."

Clint climbed from his pickup and hurried across the street.

She kept it together as they said their final goodbyes, but as she turned, she saw Micah watching from Clint's truck. She hesitated, hoping he'd give her some sign he didn't want her to go. Yeah, her luck wasn't that good.

He held her gaze for a moment then turned his head to stare straight down the street.

With a quick wave, she climbed into her car and drove down Main Street before she became a soggy mess in front of everyone. She'd made a promise to herself the previous night. No more crying. Wishes were one thing. She could wish all she wanted that Micah loved her. Reality was an entirely different animal, and she had to deal with facts.

Time for her to become the pastry chef she'd always dreamed of and worked so hard to fulfill. As she drove past the East Hope city limits, she straightened her spine and made up her mind. No more looking back. From now on, she would look ahead and make her own decisions.

Among the layers of grief was a spark of excitement. In a little over eight hours she'd be back in Salt Lake City. The conversation she'd had with Pansy had given her a feeling of optimism.

If she could just keep her mind on Pansy and Chez Romeo and her life in Utah, maybe she wouldn't spend all her time thinking of Micah and Willa Wild.

When she stopped for fuel, she checked her cell phone again. She'd given herself a stern talking to, but of course, she hadn't listened. In her head, she knew Micah wouldn't call, but her heart insisted on the possibility.

As she put the nozzle back into the pump and screwed

on the gas cap, she felt the familiar buzzing that preceded the ring of her phone. She almost dropped it in her haste to answer. Disappointment flared as she saw the caller ID. The voice on the other end was Pansy's.

"Where are you?" Pansy's breathy Marilyn voice brought a tiny smile to Cary's face.

"Just outside of Boise. I've got a ways to go yet." She tore off the receipt and climbed into her car.

"You drive careful, you hear. I don't want you getting lost now that you're finally coming home."

"I'm never lost, Pansy. You know that." Cary climbed into the car and pulled onto the highway. "It's just sometimes I don't know where I am."

## 13

Micah thought it would be easier when Cary left town. For the three days she'd spent with Millie, he'd stayed at the ranch. He hadn't expected to see her when he'd driven into town with Clint, and the sudden jolt to his heart when she'd appeared outside of Foodtown made him wish he'd been anywhere but there.

But the days since she'd left dragged on every bit as slowly as the days he'd spent avoiding her.

Why the hell couldn't people just leave him alone? Every time he saw Clint, the man tried to talk to him about Cary. So far, he'd cut that conversation off before it got started. There was just nothing to talk about. He'd wanted to call her back, but Micah didn't trust his instincts anymore.

And to top things off, Marlene called at least once a day. She'd apologized and apologized. She'd wanted to move back home. She had grandiose plans for how they'd become a family once and for all.

When he finally got a word in, he'd told her in no uncertain terms to stay away from the ranch. Since then, he hung up when he saw her number or heard her voice.

He'd saddled his new horse this morning then taken off alone. Spending the day riding a good horse and checking cattle beat hanging around people who pitied him or wanted to use him. He was kind of slow, but he wasn't going to be a patsy for anyone—especially Marlene.

He dropped the reins on Cisco's neck and let the tired horse amble along. Warm sunshine heated his back and soothed his soul. His mind wandered to the bull he was buying in a few months. He'd scoured the country to find bloodlines that would improve his herd.

Enjoying the few minutes not thinking about Cary, he was surprised to see he was almost back to the ranch house. His pleasant interval was broken when he looked up to see Clint and Millie waiting at the barn.

As he stepped down from his horse, Clint took the reins. "We want to talk to you. You wait with Millie while I unsaddle this cayuse."

Micah grabbed the reins from Clint's hand. "I can unsaddle my own horse. I've been doing it since I was ten."

Clint just smiled. "We'll go with you."

"You've become an expert at avoiding us," Millie said, falling into step beside him.

"The way you two have been hovering around me, I'm not doing a very good job." As Micah pulled off his saddle and blanket, Clint and Millie settled on the bench by the tack room. He'd been so careful to sneak away by himself this morning. Then he'd blundered right into this ambush.

After he put Cisco into the paddock, he turned and leaned against the fence. "What do you want?" Might as well get this over with.

"We want to know when you're going to get your head

out of your ass," Millie said. Her grin took some of the sting out of her words. "You've locked yourself up out here since Marlene screwed you over."

"She was a snake. You made a mistake." Clint pulled his ball cap off his head, ran his hand through his hair then slipped the cap back on. "Cary isn't Marlene."

Micah gave Clint his best mind-your-own business glare. Of course he knew Cary wasn't Marlene. That didn't mean he could trust her.

"Don't give me that look." Clint stood. "She'd never hurt you or Willa. She was leaving when she thought that guy might have found out she was here."

Micah shrugged. That thought had occurred to him, but he'd swept it away as wishful thinking.

"As opposed to Marlene, who knew her old boyfriend was well aware of where she lived, and knew she was going to hit you up for money." Millie took Micah's hand. "This is important. We don't want to see you and Willa pine away."

Micah's head jerked up. "I am not pining."

Millie looked at him for a moment before bursting into laughter. The sound of her mirth joined by Clint's bark of amusement filled the barn, but didn't do anything to lift Micah's mood. Millie waved a hand in front of her flushed face. Her laughter faded, but when she raised her gaze to his, it started all over again.

Micah stared at them, speechless. Hell, he didn't have to stay here and put up with this ridicule. He turned and stomped toward the house. At least there he could lock the door and keep them out.

A few minutes later, Micah sat on the rocker in his living room looking at Clint and Millie on the couch. So much for locking them out.

Clint had had a key to the ranch house ever since he'd been made foreman of the ranch.

"Look, we don't want to tell you what to do." Clint slapped his hands on his knees. "I wish I knew what to tell you."

"For someone who doesn't want to give me advice, you're sure full of it." Micah crossed one ankle over the other knee and rocked slowly back and forth. "This is my problem. You've both made your opinions very clear. Now can you let me figure this out on my own?"

Clint stood and took Millie's hand. As Micah rocked, he heard the front door close. Silence fell at last except for the soft squeak of the rocker. He'd missed his grandmother every day since she'd died. She'd been the one steady person in his life. Gram could always look at a situation from all angles and figure out the best way to handle it. What would she do if she were here?

He closed his eyes. A slow smile came over him as he remembered his grandmother. One thing he knew. She'd have been laughing along with Clint and Millie when he'd said he didn't pine.

"You've got to follow your heart, sonny." Her voice was so clear Micah opened his eyes and looked around to see if, by some miracle, she was here. A pang of disappointment spiked through him at the sight of the empty room. Follow his heart. To do that, he'd have to trust Cary. He'd have to risk having his heart broken.

He stood and walked to the window. The ancient Cottonwoods swayed in the breeze. One black kitten chased another across the lawn. As he watched the cattle grazing in the pasture, one thing became clear. He'd allowed Marlene to come back into their lives again and again because he didn't love her. There'd been no danger of having her hurt him. He couldn't say the same thing about Cary.

A dented Ford pickup came down the drive, clouds of dirt billowing up from the tires. The new Polaris Ranger ATV he'd bought for the ranch followed just far enough back to miss the dust. The men filed in for lunch. They hadn't complained too much about being served poorly constructed sandwiches for both the mid-day meal and dinner since Cary had left. He hoped they'd be happier with the fried chicken and potato salad he'd bought from Food-town the night before.

By the time the first ranch hand walked into the kitchen, Micah had the tubs of chicken sitting on the table. He pulled the plastic lids off the potato salad and pointed to the refrigerator. "There's Coke and sweet tea in the fridge. Help yourself."

"Thanks, boss." Toby grabbed a chicken leg then before he took a bite, he waved it at Micah. "I got just one question. When's Cary coming back?"

"Yeah," echoed Byron and Tim. "We miss her cooking."

"Don't count on that," Micah said as he hurried out the front door. He really didn't feel like explaining his personal business to his employees. The Ranger sat beside the old pickup, its shiny exterior beckoning to him. If he didn't get out of here before the men finished eating, he'd have to endure more interrogations. In the short time she'd been here, she'd wormed her way into all their hearts.

She'd become a confidant to the younger men and a friend to the guys with a few years under their belts. And she'd become more than that to him.

He climbed behind the wheel of the Ranger and took off toward the hills. He lost himself in the joy of speeding over the land and across the streams that made up the majority of his ranch. He stopped at the top of a rise and shut off the engine.

The silence was broken only by the pinging of the engine, and the gentle breeze dancing through the Cottonwood trees. The sparse scenery helped him to relax and clear his mind. Gram's advice popped into his consciousness. "Follow your heart, Sonny."

She was the only person who'd ever called him Sonny, the only person who'd get away with that name, and she'd never steered him wrong.

Cary hadn't asked for anything. She'd done her job and been kind to his daughter and everyone she'd met. He'd been wrong about Cary, wrong about so many things. It was time to make things right.

CARY HAD BEEN BACK to work at Chez Romeo for one week—five days that had stretched into infinity. She'd been bawled out by Luigi five times in those five days and this was one time too many.

"Shut up!" Her voice rang out with unsuppressed anger.

Luigi's tirade stopped in mid word, and he stood, his mouth hanging open, his face a purplish hue.

When he sucked in a breath to most likely start a new version of the same old rant, she held up her hand. "Just shut up." This time her words were soft, but the tone brooked no argument. "You are not going to yell at me ever again. I do a great job for you. If you can't see that, I'm done." She tore off the apron from around her waist and grabbed the chef's hat off her head, stuffing them into Luigi's arms.

The sound of the heavy back door slamming on that

part of her life made her smile. She didn't have a job, but she was free. The weeks working at the Circle W taught her that loving what you do is one of the most important things in life. She didn't have time any more to put up with narcissistic assholes. She was Cary Crockett, and she'd make her own life now.

The few blocks walk from the restaurant to the apartment she shared with Pansy gave her time to calm down. As she mounted the stairs to the second floor of the old Victorian, doubts crept into her mind. Her hand shook as she entered what had become when arriving back in town. Time to tell Pansy what she'd done.

"He threw another fit?" Pansy stood three steps away across the tiny living room, her arms crossed and a frown on her face. The black Cleopatra wig she wore today swung around her shoulders, the tiny gold beads woven into the braids accentuating the movement. "Jerk!"

When Cary flopped onto the ancient sofa Pansy had gotten at Goodwill, the worn leather creaked in protest. She shrugged. "I quit."

Pansy's loud shriek filled the miniscule apartment. She grabbed Cary's hands and drew her up into a dance. "You're my hero, Cary," she cried as she whirled around the room. Two steps one-way then two steps the other.

The celebration had them both laughing. She should have been worried, but the memory of Luigi standing there like a red-faced loon had her laughing so hard she had trouble breathing. Within a few short moments the laughter faded away, and the apartment became quiet.

Cary sank onto the sofa and leaned her head against the back. She turned and looked at her best friend in the world. "What am I going to do now?"

Pansy didn't hesitate for a moment. "You're going to open

your own pastry shop, and I'm going to help. Let Luigi do without both of us."

Cary watched as Pansy's angel face beneath the wig broke into a smile. Pansy had so much confidence in her, much more than Cary had in herself. Opening a pastry shop had been Cary's dream. An unattainable dream for the most part. "How will I get the money? I barely have enough to keep me until I find another job."

"Pfftt!" Pansy waved a hand in Cary's direction. "You are such a worry-wart. Things will work out."

Cary's excitement melted. Things didn't work out just because you believed. If that was so, she'd be at the Circle W with Micah, and she'd be holding Willa Wild. "I don't know."

Pansy looked at her, understanding lighting her expression. "You don't know what he'll do." She reached out and took Cary's hand.

"I do know. He thinks I could have gotten his daughter hurt or killed. I'd never do that, but if he can't see who I am, there's nothing I can do." Cary stood and walked into the kitchen. "Want a beer?"

"Sure." Pansy followed her and popped the tops on two cans of Old Milwaukee beer while Cary sliced a lime.

Even with the added citrus flavor, this cut-rate beer wasn't anything like Corona, but when you're broke, you make do with what you can afford.

Pansy lifted her can and tinked it against Cary's. "Here's to us. Starting tomorrow, we'll conquer the world."

Cary lifted her bottle in a half-hearted toast and took a drink. "Do you really think we can open a business?"

"You've got the money Ken didn't walk away with, and I have set some aside. What better to use it for than this?" Pansy set her beer on the counter and pulled a tablet out of the drawer. "We'll make a list. Things we need to do. First is to work up a business plan."

Three hours later, they had the basics but were no closer to finding the remaining money to start the business. "I don't know how this is going to work."

"Positive thoughts here, Cary."

At the sound of a knock on the door, Pansy handed the pencil to Cary. "I'll get that. Probably Luigi begging us to come back."

Cary heard muffled voices as she tried to come up with enticing ideas that would convince a banker to loan start-up money. To hell with enticing, she couldn't even come up with boring ideas.

Pansy looked around the corner and waved to get her attention. "It's for you. I think it might be important." Her usually expressive face was blank.

Cary gave her a quizzical look then put the pencil on the pad and stood. "Who is it?"

"You'll have to see for yourself."

Cary had had about all the bad news she could handle for a lifetime. If this was more, she was checking out and not leaving a forward address. She rounded the corner then stopped in her tracks. Micah stood on the stoop, his black Stetson in his hand.

Cary opened her mouth to speak. She'd gone over what she'd say if she ever got the chance to speak to Micah again, but she couldn't remember a word.

Pansy nudged her from behind. "I'm assuming this is your cowboy?" She pushed Cary toward the sofa and turned to Micah. "Come on in. Cary will regain her power of speech in a minute."

The apartment's living room was barely big enough for a

beat-up sofa and a small rocker. Micah's presence made it seem like a closet.

Cary knew she had to speak, if just to tell Micah to leave. "What are you doing here? Is Willa Wild okay?" Her heart raced at the thought of something happening to the little girl.

"She's fine." His deep voice stroked her skin. "Cary, I need to talk to you about something."

Pansy jumped up off the couch and grabbed her sweater from the hook on the wall. "I'd like to visit with you both, but I have a job to quit." Before Cary could ask her to stay and act like a buffer, her roommate was out the door.

She couldn't make eye contact with Micah. Her head spun, and her hands shook.

"Breathe, Cary." He moved across the room to stand in front of her. "I'm sorry. I should have trusted you."

The rushing sound in her ears sounded like a day at a wind-blown beach. She raised her gaze from his worn boots to his green eyes. Had she heard him right? Even if he'd apologized, it didn't mean he wanted her around on a permanent basis. Righteous anger burbled up from her center, and she stood, forcing him to take a step back. "You should have."

He reached out and touched her cheek with his fingers. "I know that now. Forgive me, Cary. I promise to trust you from now to forever."

"Can you do that? Trust me?" He was saying the things she'd longed to hear, but did he mean them? "How do I know?"

Micah took another step closer, so close she could feel the delicious heat coming off his body. He tilted her head up so they looked in each other's eyes. In slow motion, he lowered his head and kissed her. When he pulled back, he placed his palm against her cheek. "You'll have to trust me when I say I love you."

There were no guarantees in this life, but this man wasn't Ken. She'd trusted Micah since the first time she'd seen him. Her heart could still be broken, but Micah was the best bet she'd ever met. It was time to make a hard decision, to play it safe or fly.

Well, she'd always envied eagles.

# EPILOGUE

Pansy carried the giant platter of hand-decorated cupcakes out to the front porch of the ranch house. Cary followed with a plate of Key Lime cookies and another of luscious, double chocolate brownies. The two women had spent several days baking sweets for the party. Sweet tea and water sat in cut glass pitchers that had belonged to Micah's grandmother, and the beer and pop were in ice chests on the lawn.

Micah had insisted they invite all of East Hope, and Cary agreed.

Millie climbed out of Clint's truck and hurried to the porch. "Let me see." She grabbed Cary's hand and tilted it back and forth to see the facets of the diamond shine in the light. "It's beautiful."

Cary looked at the ring. "It was Micah's grandmother's. It is pretty, isn't it?" Her smile was so wide she felt kind of silly, but there was no way she could stop.

Millie put her arm around Cary's shoulders. "What about Marlene? Has she been back?" With her free hand, she grabbed a couple of cookies. "Mmmm, did you make these? You've got to give me the recipe. No, no, I don't cook very well. How about you make me some once a week. I might even sell them in the store."

Cary laughed. No only had she found Micah and Willa Wild, she found wonderful new friends and a town to call her own. "Marlene came over the first day I was back. Micah told her we were getting married. He also told her she'd need to make an appointment before coming to the ranch again."

Millie snorted.

Cary couldn't help laughing with her friend. "She wasn't a happy camper. I think she thought she could maneuver Micah like she always had, but he took her arm and led her to her car then walked away."

Willa Wild came running across the yard. "Cary, can we have some cupcakes to take to the fort?" She hopped from one foot to the other, her beautiful face flushed with excitement. The neighbor kids were here for the day, and Micah had finished her tree fort.

Cary took a paper plate and filled it with cupcakes. She placed a pile of napkins on the top, not that the kids would use them. "Have fun, sweetie."

Cary looked up from Willa to see Micah watching her from across the yard. He excused himself from the men he was talking to and headed toward her.

"Having fun?" He gazed down at her, his smile warming her heart. He took her hand and touched the ring. "This looks good on you. Grams would be proud."

"I hope so." She slid her fingers through his, relishing the touch of this man.

"I love you."

"I love y—" Before Cary could get the words out, Willa came running, tears streaming down her face and frosting streaked down her T-shirt.

"I dropped the-the c-cupcakes, Pa." She threw her arms around Micah's legs then lifted her dirt-streaked face to Cary. "I didn't mean to, but Blake was teasing me about being slow, and I wanted to show him."

Cary knelt beside the little girl who'd become her daughter. She looked up at Micah and mouthed *I love you.* Then she turned back to Willa Wild.

"Honey, in this life, good things happen and bad things happen. There's not much we can do about that, but no matter what, there's always more cupcakes."

∼

*Readers are the icing on an author's cake.*
*Thank you for taking the time to read*
*Gimme Some Sugar.*
*If you liked Cary and Micah's story, you'll love Sweet Cowboy*
*Kisses, the second in my*
*Sugar Coated Cowboys series.*

∼

*Sweet Cowboy Kisses*
*Book 2, Sugar Coated Cowboys*

*Is Forgiveness their real super-power?*
*He rides the baddest bulls...*
*She's a temptress in a Cleopatra wig...*
*To attain his dream, Kade Vaughn must ride the toughest bulls on*
*the circuit. There's only one glitch. Now the cowboy's on a forced*
*vacation at his friends' ranch.*
*To get through each day, Pansy Lark pretends to be other women*

*through cosplay. Famous, strong women who took what they wanted from life. She lost it all, but she's not that weak girl anymore.*

*Can sweet cowboy kisses heal her wounded heart? If you love resilient women and rodeo cowboys that are all heart, get Sweet Cowboy Kisses today.*

*All of the the men and women of East Hope, Oregon can be found in one spot in my Sugar Coated Cowboys four-book box set.*

# ABOUT THE AUTHOR

Stephanie Berget was born loving horses, a ranch kid trapped in a city girl's body. It took her twelve years to convince her parents she needed a horse of her own. She developed a lifelong love of rodeo when she married her own, hot cowboy. She and the Bronc Rider traveled throughout the Northwest while she ran barrels and her cowboy rode bucking horses. She started writing to put a realistic view of rodeo and ranching into western romance. Stephanie and her husband live on a farm located along the Oregon/Idaho border. They raise hay, horses and cattle, with the help of Dizzy Dottie, the Border Collie and Cisco, barrel and team roping horse extraordinaire.

Stephanie is delighted to hear from readers. Reach her at http://www.stephanieberget.com